Paws of the Yeti

Blue Moon Investigations

Book 10

Steve Higgs

Dedication

This book is dedicated to several fans that have helped bring it into being.

My thanks go to Mike Woods, Robin Hansen, Sherril Beaston, and Joann K for coming up with the name for this book. I asked the question and had many hundreds of suggestions, but these four all came up with Paws of the Yeti and it was my favourite by far since it captures the fun nature of the story.

Also in need of a very special mention, are some super fans that helped me to create the characters.

Hotel owner and Tempest's client - Hubert Caron suggested by Karen Bennett
Central female - Priscille Peran suggested by Liz Jennings
Rival Hotel owner - Gerard Chevalier suggested by June Brewer
Rival Hotel owner's son - Gils Chevalier suggested by June Brewer
Police chief - Francois Delacroix suggested by Nancy Buntrock

The level of detail provided for some of the characters even went as far as favourite foods and sporting achievements at school. Honestly, I think some of the people that read my books should be writing themselves.

If you want to know how to join in the fun and get your name on the dedication page of a future publication, please see the next page where you will find a link to my newsletter service.

Table of Contents

Free Books and More

I had been hiding in the bushes for almost an hour already. It wasn't the first time in my life I had set an ambush, previously though I had always been armed, and my military career had occurred at a time when Iraq and Afghanistan were centre stage so I had generally not had to combat the cold as well. Today though, it was hovering around zero. Cold enough to be cold but not so cold that one had to be wary of exposure. There were children playing in the play park in front of me as a demonstration that any acknowledgement of the cold was more an acknowledgement of weakness on my part.

I was watching the play park, the cold getting to me only because I was doing my best to remain motionless. I was at the end of a case, or at least I hoped I was. A group of mums had hired me after their children reported being scared by a creature when they were out playing.

The first part of my investigation had been to interview some of the children. Naturally, I had wondered if the creature would prove to be a clever story dreamt up by the children, but I found them to be quite traumatised by their experience. It made me angry to see such innocent faces so confused about what they had seen. Unanimously, they described the creature they had seen as a hairy, brown monster. It had glowing red eyes and horns and big tusks that jutted from its bottom jaw. Some of the kids had drawn the creature, the childish scrawls sufficiently similar for me to believe this was not made up.

I had seen people traumatised by their experiences before. Men and women who had volunteered to go to awful places and see awful things. They were always quiet, withdrawn, struggling to process the information indelibly ingrained in their heads and the kids were the same.

So, here I was, hiding under a bush, watching children play and feeling guilty that I was using them as bait. I had been trying to catch this guy for two weeks although I had put the case on hold when my father had been injured. His case had been a higher priority for a few days but I had gone back to this as soon as I had been able. Unfortunately, there wasn't much to go on. The creature, whatever it was, had targeted six different play grounds starting just over two months ago. It might have gone back further than that, but I was dealing with the reports that I had, not those I could imagine. He usually arrived without warning, leaping out to scare the children senseless and then disappearing again before the adults could catch up with him/it.

My assumption was that it was a man in a costume. It always was. Vampires, ghosts, zombies; none of it was real. I had never believed it was, however, there were a lot of people that did, and they hired me when they heard a bump in the night and needed someone to explain what it was. In this case, it wasn't a bump in the night, it was a creep in a costume and I was going to tear him a new one when I caught him.

I couldn't keep the children out much longer and it had taken a considerable amount of convincing to have the parents send their children out here tonight. Short on clues, it was my most proactive move to set the creep a trap and let him walk into it. I just hoped he would turn up because I wasn't sure the parents would agree to it twice. Time was ticking on though and I would soon have to accept that he wasn't coming. Then I saw movement to my right.

I watched, squinting to see if the dark shape I had seen moving through the shadows was really there. My eyes hadn't been deceived though, there was something in the trees on the other side of the field. Was it watching the kids? That would be typical creep behaviour. I wriggled my fingers and toes, needing to make sure that my body was still operational and not asleep. The spot I was squinting at was less than fifty feet from the kids in the playground. I did not want them to see it, but I did want to be able to honestly report that I had intercepted the creep on his way to scare the children. I was closer to it than it was to the children. I could beat it to them if I moved fast enough but I waited for it to emerge from the shadows before showing myself. The last thing I wanted was to tip it off to my presence, send it scurrying away and lose it. If I waited just a little bit longer, it would be in the open where there was no hope of escape.

A few more seconds elapsed. Then it happened. The creature emerged into the moonlight, exposing itself. It was exactly as the children had drawn, a shaggy brown coat of fur with an ugly head topped with horns and glowing eyes. Its focus was firmly on the playpark ahead of it and whatever it had planned would not be conducive to the children there sleeping soundly tonight.

Show time.

As the creature took its first step toward the children, I burst from the bushes, accelerating into a sprint as I crossed the short space between us. Tempted to roar a battle cry, I kept silent lest I draw the children's attention to the creature now advancing upon them. However, I was about to start a fight with what looked a monster/alien from an old episode of Dr Who and the occasion deserved a token attempt at a cool one-liner.

As I came in front of it, I raised my hands and said, 'You shall not pass.'

Whether the idiot in the costume even got the reference I would never find out, but the head of the beast turned toward me, its expression unchanged of course because a fake face cannot show surprise, but I was willing to bet the face inside the mask was shocked as I dropped my shoulder, caught it just above the hips and lifted it clean off the ground.

I drove it back a dozen feet, taking it off the path and back into the shadows. I couldn't tell if the kids had seen anything, or their parents for that matter but I had to focus on the task at hand right now. I could worry about the kids in a minute.

The person inside the costume was a lot lighter than me, I registered this as the darkness away from the path enveloped us once more. I wasn't expecting there to be much of a fight, but one never could tell. However, as we hit the ground, the creature was beneath me, so my shoulder slammed into its gut and I heard its breath shoot out. It was instantly winded, but I didn't leave it at that; I rolled over forwards, letting my momentum carry me until I was back on my feet. Bouncing onto the balls of my feet, I was just beyond the head piece which I had grabbed as I turned. The fur was so obviously artificial under my fingers that I felt no hesitation as I twisted it first one way and then the other and then ripped it clean off.

Then, I was standing over the man inside the suit, looking down at him as I judged whether he was going to fight or surrender. He was a balding man in his early twenties with a sheen of sweat on his scalp. His face was contorted in utter panic. Any thoughts he might have had of fleeing, and any concern I had that he might try to fight, were instantly dispelled by some of the children's parents arriving next to me. They had seen the brief scuffle I guess and had started running at that point.

The man on the ground said nothing. He knew he was beaten.

'Would you be so kind as to call the police, please?' I asked the man nearest me. I wanted my hands free just in case the man did try anything. While the dad made a phone call, I knelt next to the Fiddler. It was the nickname I had given him at the start of the case because he was targeting kiddies. Thankfully, all the moron had ever done was leap out and scare the children but who knew what he might advance to if he hadn't been caught. 'Do you want to give me your name?' I asked.

He shook his head and remained tight-lipped. However, he placed his right hand against the grass to push himself upright. I placed a hand on his shoulder as I said, 'Stay there, please. The police will be here soon.' It had been the wrong thing to say as the Fiddler decided he wanted to be gone by the time the police arrived. Instantly thrashing about to escape me, he was able to throw my hand off as he rolled onto his front to get up.

The circle of parents, who had now been joined by some of their braver children, all took a pace back but any worry they might have felt vanished as soon as I could have arisen when I sat on his back. 'It's a good costume,' I acknowledged. 'Where did you get it?' He didn't answer, just thrashed his head around trying to look at me. 'Come on. What harm can it do?' I encouraged. It really was a well-conceived costume, the horns and tusks on the head quite real-looking.

'eBay,' he mumbled quietly. 'It's an old prop from Dr Who.'

I laughed at my earlier observation about the same show. 'What episode?'

'The Horror of Milton Hall.' He twisted his head to look at me as best he could. 'Who are you, man?'

I opened my mouth to say something cool, but I was beaten to it by one of the mums, 'He's Tempest Michaels. A hero that battles creatures in the dark.' It sounded way better coming from her. I grinned at her, it seemed like the thing to do, but she winked at me and I remembered that she had been to every meeting I had with the client group and unlike the other parents, she had always been alone.

5

Single mum.

I stayed on top of the man for another ten minutes, his protests falling on deaf ears though I was glad when the flashing blue and red lights could be seen bouncing off the houses and low clouds. A pair of squad cars reached the end of the street nearest the play park then mounted the curb and drove across the grass toward us, a parent guiding them.

Only as the uniformed officers approached did I clamber off the man in the costume. Then began the process of giving statements and wrapping up which always takes longer than I think it should. Most of the parents drifted away but oddly the single mum hung around and didn't even have a child with her.

It was after six when the police left with the man in cuffs on the back seat. He was still in his costume, it was evidence, though they may have left it on because he was naked beneath it; I hadn't thought to ask him. Heading back to my car, it was impossible to avoid the single mum that had been waiting for me for more than an hour.

She was smiling at me, positioned so that I had to pass her to get to my car. 'All done then,' I said.

'Yes. Well done,' she remarked. 'I don't suppose we will see him again.' Then she bit her lip, thinking about what she wanted to say next. Her intention was obvious, and my response was already worked out, but I couldn't think how to say, "No, thank you." before she asked me a question. 'Are you... would you like to come for a drink?' she asked. She was smiling shyly at me in a cute and quite endearing way, but even if I hadn't already been dating the world's most attractive woman, I would have turned her down.

Gently, I said, 'Sorry, I'm already with someone.'

She nodded, disappointed but maybe not surprised as if she had been expecting the answer I gave. 'Okay,' she said. 'Thank you for tonight.'

'Thank you for hiring me.'

The lady walked away, back to one of the houses on the estate that bordered the play park and I got into my car. I was cold, the layers of my clothing only doing so much to keep the cold at bay. It had long since penetrated deep into my hands and feet and ears. As the engine roared to life and I waited for the heat to start thawing me out, I checked my phone.

I had a stack of missed calls. All from Jagjit. As I moved my finger toward the green button to call him back, the phone jumped to life in my hand. I had an incoming call. This one from Hilary. Hilary never called me.

I answered, 'Good evening, buddy. What's up?'

'Hi, Tempest.' Hilary spoke rapidly as if the message was important. 'Jagjit called me. He's been trying to get hold of you for hours,' he explained.

'I've been on a bust, dealing with the police and stuff. I was just about to call him. Did he say why he was calling?' I asked.

'Yes! He has a case for you in France. Or rather he has a client with a case. There's a yeti on the loose!'

In the car on the way back to my house, I thumbed the button to connect the phone and said the name of the person I wanted to speak to. I got no answer from Jagjit though, so I tried the next person I wanted.

Moments later, Big Ben's voice burst over the speaker. 'Hey, butt muppet, what are you up to?'

'Good evening, Ben,' I replied. 'How do you fancy a few days skiing?'

'Skiing?'

'Yes.'

'When?'

'As soon as you can pack.'

'Sounds groovy, but why the rush?'

'I got a message from Jagjit. There is a Yeti in Tignes. There is a client there who wants to hire me to investigate it, it would seem.'

At the other end, I could hear Big Ben laughing. 'A Yeti? Some moron in a costume then. Solve the case, spread some seed around the lovely snow bunnies hanging out at the slopes and get some ski time in. Sounds like a party.'

'Well, there's an overnight train that leaves in four hours. Can you be ready by then?' I asked.

I could hear his cogs turning. 'I have a couple of dates to cancel, but there will be plenty of women where we are going. Sure, I just need to dig my ski gear out of storage and pack a few things. You gonna pick me up?'

'In my car? No, we'll have to take yours to get to the station with all the gear in it.' I loved my two-seater Porsche, but I had to admit that it wasn't exactly practical unless one wanted to go fast.

'Ok, count me in,' he said. 'I'll be around your place in a couple of hours.' We disconnected and I tried Jagjit again.

This time it connected, his familiar voice saying, 'Tempest, you're a hard man to get hold of.'

'I was on a case,' I explained. 'I understand you have a Yeti problem in Tignes.'

'It's not Tignes, actually. It's a small exclusive resort not far from Tignes called Harvarti but I guess it comes under Tignes because there is nothing here other than the hotels, a few shops and restaurants and the ski centre. Anyway, a woman was killed yesterday; the daughter of the owner of the hotel we are staying in and another woman who was with her was hurt. He announced a €50000.00 reward for its capture, but I figured this was right up your street.'

Questions were lining up in my head. I was going to have to write a list before I started forgetting them, but a couple instantly jumped to the front of the queue, 'Is the owner looking to hire me, or is this just about the reward?'

'I did mention that I knew a paranormal investigator and showed him your webpage. He asked me to make contact with you. You might want to call him yourself though before you set off.' My brain was running fast, I had a lot to consider but my first thought was that I wanted to go skiing. During my time in the Army there had been semi-regular opportunities to take to the slopes, they encouraged adventurous activities and subsidised it for those that went. We didn't get taught to ski backwards while firing a machine gun like you see in the James Bond movies though. Instead, in

9

between the fun stuff where we got taught to ski, we had to participate in survival training where we would dig holes in the snow and spend the night not dying from the cold because we learned how to deal with it. We also learned what cold was, something few people do because the army loved to help us test our limits.

What I said in reply was, 'I'm coming anyway. Big Ben is coming too. I'll call the hotel owner shortly and discuss the case, mostly because I don't want the man to throw away his money when it will be some fool in a Chewbacca outfit he bought online and bleached.'

'When will you get here?' Jagjit asked.

'Tomorrow late morning. We are going to take the overnight train.' A thought occurred to me. 'Are there rooms available?' It was going to be a problem if there were not.

'Yes, quite a few actually. There's a bit of a stink about a rival hotel stealing all the business. I don't know if that's true, but you won't have to worry about bunking with Big Ben.'

We talked for another couple of minutes while Jagjit gave the hotel owner's name and number, and I found out about the extent of the injured girl's wounds and whether the Yeti had been seen by anyone other than the surviving woman. Jagjit had learned about the Yeti sighting the moment they arrived at the resort. They were issuing a warning to everyone that they should not stray off the pistes; a problem no doubt for many skiers who would specifically look to explore the untouched powder available away from the safer slopes. The Yeti had been spotted by more than a dozen people, but no one had got close to it until the poor woman and her friend had strayed into the woods late yesterday when the slopes were due to close and the sun was setting.

Are Yetis nocturnal? I pondered, then caught myself and chuckled. How could I deliberate upon the likely habits of a make-believe creature?

I bid Jagjit a good evening with his bride and disconnected. During our conversation, I had run through a mental checklist of what I would need to pack, so as I pulled onto my drive and killed the engine, I was trying to remember it all and wondering if I had wax for my skis and where the heck I might have put my gloves and goggles.

I live in the small village of Finchampstead, a couple of miles outside Maidstone in the South East corner of England. We are surrounded by slopes, but they are undulating hills not mountains, so I was glad that the excellent ski resorts of the Alps were no more than a few hours to get to by car. It was too far to be a practical weekend destination, but easily driveable in a day. Trains ran there overnight, the time of the next one had been the very first thing I had checked, but now I wondered if we might be better off just driving.

My front door barked as I got to it, the two Dachshunds on the other side excited to see me and wanting their dinner. I greeted them with, 'Hey, guys,' as they climbed my legs and did their best to block my way in.

Dozer rolled onto his back as I took to a knee to fuss them, their demand for attention was fleeting though. I had been out of the house for a few hours so they wanted to visit the garden and then they would very much want their dinner; it was a well-practised routine.

As they dashed across the lawn for a reason only known to them, I asked the air, 'What do I do with you two?' I pretty much universally took them everywhere with me when I could. My only concern with taking them to the Alps was the cold. They were tiny dogs and prone to feeling the cold. I could leave them with my parents as my mum and dad loved having them to visit, but I couldn't say how long I would be away, and it

11

seemed likely I could conduct the case even with them in tow. It was settled then; the dogs were coming on a ski holiday too.

While they snuffled outside, and the kettle boiled some water for tea, I jotted a list of things to pack on a handy pad I kept for writing my grocery needs. Then I remembered there was another person I needed to call – Amanda Harper.

I had met Amanda Harper on a misty morning ten weeks ago and had been instantly attracted to her. The attraction had turned to infatuation and if I am honest it had been a problem for me that I had struggled to control. While I was lusting after her, she saw me as a potential employer and had asked for a job at a time when I knew I needed to take someone on. Working together though had created a barrier to my desires, not opened a door, and she had been dating someone else while I tried to quell my thoughts for her by dating others.

Then we had both found ourselves single and without partners at Jagjit's wedding just three days ago and the magic had happened. I had admitted my feelings for her, and she had kissed me. Several times. I had a room at the wedding venue, but we didn't fall straight into bed as some couples might. Instead, we had talked for several hours, tucked away in the corner of the reception and laughed about how rubbish we had both been about getting together. The following day we had met for coffee and had kissed again. We were in no rush to get to the next stage, although I will admit that Mr Wriggly was getting very impatient and threatening strike action if something didn't happen soon.

We had dinner planned for tomorrow night, both of us taking things slow by mutual agreement because we worked together and knew that getting this wrong would make continuing to work together difficult. Now though, I was off to France and needed to postpone our next date. I had no concern that this would upset her, but it did occur to me that she might want to come along.

The dogs barked at the back door, their tiny claws propelling them across the carpet and through to the kitchen once I opened the door enough for them to wedge their heads through it. As they chowed down their dinner, I picked up my phone again and called Amanda.

As she answered, she said, 'Hi, Tempest, what's up? How did the Fiddler bust go?' Her voice always sounded like a choir of angels singing to me.

'It was an easy bust, thank you. The clients were very happy, and the kids didn't see a thing.' We had discussed the concept of using the kids as bait when I was trying to work out how to catch the Fiddler. It didn't sit well with either of us, but neither could devise a plan that would work better.

'Oh, good,' she replied, then fell silent while she waited for me to say why I had called.

I got on with asking my question, but did so in a round about way, 'I, um, need to cancel our date tomorrow night. Something has come up.'

'Oh. Okay.' I could hear the surprise mixed with disappointment she was trying to hide.

'I wondered, actually, if you might like to have our next date in France?' I let that hang for a second so she could process it, but spoke again before she had a chance to. 'There's a Yeti at the resort Jagjit and Alice are staying in. It killed a woman yesterday.'

'A yeti? You mean some moron in a costume.' It was exactly what Big Ben had said. 'Are you going straight out there?'

'That's the plan,' I admitted. 'Big Ben and I are going but it could be a lucrative case and I am guessing that it won't take long once we work out who stands to gain.' I dropped the timbre of my voice, deliberately giving it a husky, bedroom tone, 'I have visions of log fires and schnapps to keep us warm after a day on the slopes. We can take a couple of days for ourselves once the case is solved. It's supposed to be spectacular there.'

Amanda sighed. 'I can't say I am not tempted. I need to finish the case I am on though. I couldn't possible leave now, the clients need me.'

I scrunched my face in disappointment. However, I wasn't surprised that she wouldn't drop the case she was on for a few days away; her diligence and determination were factors I had wanted when I employed her. Like me, she did as she ought, not as she wanted.

I had her tell me about the case she was on and wished her luck closing it swiftly. My offer would stay open if she could get to France before I was done. We bade goodnight to each other, each wishing the other luck and expressing a hope to see each other soon. I placed my phone back on the kitchen counter and took a swig of tea. I was disappointed that I would not see Amanda for a few days but told myself to shut up and get on with it. I would see her soon enough.

And she had better be naked!

Mr Wriggly's thoughts aside, I was looking forward to the relationship evolving. I couldn't think about that now though. I had to pack for France.

There wasn't much to look at or anywhere to go on the Eurostar car train. Specifically designed to take people in their cars from England to France or vice-versa in just over half an hour; the carriages were little more than a series of car parking spaces one after the other for the length of the train. There was no bar or snack shack; the only concession was toilets set every few carriages.

Though it was only a short journey on the train, I got the dogs out of the car anyway. We were in for a long drive overnight, which Big Ben and I would share, and the dogs would sleep in their bed that was on top of some bags on the back seat. I doubted we would hear from them at any point, but it was prudent to make them stretch their legs now.

Big Ben got out as well, spotted two women in the car behind us which was also loaded up with ski gear, and went to talk them out of their knickers. Big Ben drove a shiny black, huge, kitted-out Ford Ranger utility vehicle with a truckman cab over the load bed. He had money to spare so had coughed up the extra to add the Deranged body kit which flared the wheel arches, then added twenty-inch wheels and put a massive bulge on the bonnet. It looked like the car that Batman might drive if he wanted to go cross-country. I couldn't deny the practicality though. We had fitted four pairs of skis, two each because it's nice to have some choice, plus boots, helmets, bags of clothing, plus all the gear that the dogs needed and a holdall that Big Ben assured me was full of condoms and would be coming back empty. Putting all of that in had barely dented the available load space though there was already a vague plan to bring back several cases of French wine when we returned.

While I walked the little dogs up and down the carriage we were in, I thought back to my conversation with the owner of the Constantine Hotel, a man who was now my client. Hubert Caron was managing a lot of conflicting emotions, that was evident to me in the first few seconds of listening to him speak. He was gravely upset about his daughter's death, angry about several things including his daughter's death, and he was ready to blame the owner of the other hotel in the resort. I had outlined my fees, but he had scoffed at the costs. I guess if you own and run a luxury hotel in an exclusive resort, you probably don't have too many cash concerns, although he did express that he was being squeezed out of business by his rival and the Yeti was the latest problem in a long line of issues that had blighted his hotel in recent times.

My stroll with the dogs had taken me to the far end of the carriage. There were doors to lead me through to the next carriage but no reason to go any further when it would look exactly the same as this one. I walked behind the rearmost car and started back up the other side. I could see Big Ben ahead of me, leaning against the wall of the carriage while grinning lazily at the two ladies who had now left their car and joined him. They both had their backs to me as they faced him but turned to see what he was looking at as he chucked a wave in my direction.

It was a tactic on his part because he knew girls, in general, went mad for my dogs. These two were no exception. I estimated their age to be late twenties or perhaps early thirties, they were both slim and attractive and of Asian descent although I would struggle to pin point a region or country. Chances were they had lived in England their entire lives.

The first one to spot Bull and Dozer was closest to the car, her hip leaning against the driver's door. She glanced, did a double take and as her eyes widened, she tapped her friend on the arm. 'Look, Maisy. Look at the sausages.'

Maisy turned her head and then turned around completely and crouched to make cooing noises while the two boys struggled against their leads. I kept them in check, but we got there soon enough. With

16

their tails wagging so fast they were barely visible; the dogs accepted the affection the ladies were offering as if they were continually starved of it living with me.

Above the ladies' heads, Big Ben was gesticulating at me. I took his actions to be a question: Which one do I want?

I mouthed, 'Neither,' silently while shaking my head in despair. That he knew I was with Amanda now, and would consider even the slightest exchange of affection with another woman as cheating, never entered his equation. He and I were very different in some respects.

He saw my response though and laughed at me, saying out loud, 'All the more for me then, wet pants.'

'All the more what?' asked Maisy as she stood back up again. Then turning to me she said, 'Your dogs are delightful,' with a smile.

'What are their names?' asked her friend, which gave me cause to talk about the dogs for the next couple of minutes. As I finished regaling them with Dozer's adventure in the river a couple of months back, the tannoy pinged followed by an announcement that we were just a few minutes from arriving and a request that all passengers now return to their cars.

'It was nice meeting you,' said Maisy as she stepped to her car and opened the driver's door. Her friend said the same and they were gone leaving Big Ben looking confused.

Cheerily I called out, 'Come on, Ben. There will be girls where we are going.' I slid between the cars to get around to the passenger side. He stomped along grumpily to settle behind the wheel while I tucked the dogs back into their bed. With a final pat, I pulled a blanket over them and joined Big Ben in the cab. 'You look unusually irked at losing your prey,' I observed.

He turned his head toward me. 'I am behind on my quota,' he replied dryly.

I had to laugh. 'Do you mean you have been getting less than usual?'

'Yes. Last week the cleaning activities at the Dockyard, Jagjit's stag do, where you refused to let me bring strippers, and then the wedding all conspired to rob me of opportunity. I'm not complaining about sorting out the business at the Dockyard and helping out your dad,' he was holding his hands up defensively, 'but I am behind on my monthly quota and plan to catch up this week.'

'Didn't you hook up with no fewer than three of Alice's friends at the wedding?'

'Yup,' he admitted happily.

'And didn't you invite a bus load of beauties to Jagjit's stag do anyway. Surely one of them must have gone home with you.'

'Two of them,' he boasted.

'And yet you claim to be behind on your quota?'

'Indeed.' The traffic ahead of us was starting to move. Big Ben turned his engine on and waited for the car in front. I genuinely didn't want to know anymore about it. I would be quite content if I got to a point where Amanda and I engaged in nocturnal activities on a semi-regular basis. Relationships were, in my experience, quite hot at the start until the fire of passion burned down a bit. I was looking forward to both stages.

With that thought in my head, I settled into the seat and got comfortable. Big Ben was going to drive the first shift and wake me when he got tired. It would take between six and seven hours to get to Tignes where we had to abandon the car and take a cable car to the resort. I was going to get some sleep.

It was still dark out when I opened my eyes, but the first tinges of daylight could be seen on the horizon as we travelled east. I smacked my lips a few times as I squinted at the clock on the dash and stretched in place. Driving might have been the easiest and fastest solution, but it wasn't the most comfortable even in Big Ben's giant car.

Big Ben's hand swung in front of my face with a fast food chain soda cup in it. 'Some caffeine?' he asked.

I yawned and accepted the cup. My tongue felt like it was coated in glue. 'Where are we?' I asked as I sat myself up straight in the chair.

Big Ben glanced at the centre console in which his satnav was tracking our position. 'About fifty kilometres from Tignes.'

'I thought you were going to wake me up,' I said around another yawn.

He looked across at me. 'I might have but you were out of it. I stopped for gas twice and walked the dogs and made sure they had a drink and I stopped for some food. I got you some thinking you would wake up...'

'Where is it?' I asked, suddenly hungry and ready to eat even if it was cold.

'But you didn't, so I ate if for you.'

Nuts.

'Besides, I said I would wake you up when I got tired.' He broke off what he was saying to yawn deeply, then pointed to his face. 'You see that? That's the first yawn all night. You've only been awake two minutes and you are already boring me to sleep.'

I rolled my eyes. He was such a dick.

20

'So, you want me to take over?' I asked.

'Nearly there now. I might as well finish it.' He checked his rear-view mirror and pulled out to go around a truck. 'You will want to find the client when we arrive, yes?' I nodded. 'Then I will get a few hours shut eye when we get there.'

That seemed to be the plan settled so I checked on the dogs, gave each a pat and relaxed in the passenger seat for the rest of the drive. Just a couple of minutes later, Big Ben flicked his indicator on and left the motorway. We were heading into the mountains, the remaining kilometres much slower going as the road wound around and around to make the climb manageable. Jagjit had told me the region had enjoyed an early drop of snow. There was snow at this altitude most of the year of course, but it fell far less frequently through the summer and autumn which reduced all but the highest pistes to impassable icefields. A good drop of snow changed that overnight and there was more on the way he assured me.

We passed attractive, colourful billboards advertising the ski regions ahead. Memories of previous ski trips, of the majestic scenery and of hurtling downhill at life-threatening speeds. Memories of the apres-ski and fun evenings with army buddies. Snowy mountain ranges held a romantic place in my heart, and I was excited to be heading back to the slopes after too long away from them.

We started passing buildings and the snow was getting deeper as we continued up. The roads were clear, the success of all the businesses above the snow line depending on it, but there was very little traffic, probably due to the time of day and we made good time.

'That looks like it there,' I pointed. Ahead was a sign advertising the Harvarti cable car. Beyond it I could see the cable car itself and a large car park for the thousands of guests the resort must hold at peak season. It was less than half full now.

With the car parked, Big Ben and I grabbed extra layers we had stashed in a handy location knowing we would need them when we arrived. The dogs would need to pee but would not like the cold one bit. They wagged their tails at me in excitement though since the humans were doing stuff and it was breakfast time. I stuffed them into onesies I had bought a long time ago when they had been on sale thinking they might prove handy one day. Both were fleece lined and came down to the ankle of each paw. The only bits exposed were the bits I needed them to make stuff come out of but even with the extra layer they would not tolerate the cold for long; their big flappy ears would freeze in no time if left exposed. They were good dogs though, both sensing the need to be quick about it when I placed them on the snowy ground. While I attended to them, Big Ben walked across to the ticket office to find out when the cable car would start to operate.

He came jogging back as the dogs were eating their breakfast in the passenger's footwell. 'We can go in ten minutes. Apparently, the client owns the cable car and told them to expect us.'

So, ten minutes later, with bags and ski gear loaded into a compartment behind the main carriage and the dogs on my lap staring out of the window in doggy wonder, the cable car pulled out and began its ascent. We were already well up into the snow of the mountains. Where snow ploughs had mounded it to the side of the road it was several feet high, and in the car park, where cars had arrived before the most recent drop, there was eight inches of fresh snow on their roofs.

The cable car lifted us high above the houses as it tracked a path up the mountainside toward the ski slopes above Tignes. The whole region was a series of linked ski resorts, the largest of which is Val-d'Isère. One of the big attractions for winter sports fans was the ability to almost never ski the same slope twice. Complex routes could be devised so the skier or snowboarder could range down slope and up ski-lift for hours, going from one end of the resorts to the other and back. We passed over the top of many exciting-looking runs as we made our way to the crest of a mountain. The cable car didn't stop at the top though, as we broached the summit, the wide expanse of the Alps was revealed before us, a huge range of snow-topped peaks poking up through the early morning mist like shark fins above the water. Then the cable car descended slightly, and the mist engulfed us once more.

On my lap, Dozer wagged a confused and nervous tail a few times. I couldn't tell what might be going through his little canine brain, but I was certain he had never witnessed anything like the view I had just shown him. I smooshed him under my chin for comfort before settling him back on my lap.

When we emerged from the mist fifteen minutes later, we could see our final destination shining in the sun ahead of us. Harvarti cable car station had been architecturally designed from glass and chrome with a white roof that resembled honeycomb. It was free of snow, which was undoubtedly achieved by passing heat through it, but I had to acknowledge how impressed I always found myself when looking at buildings on the top of mountains: How on earth did they get the building materials up here? How did they get the equipment to the top of the mountain? It wasn't like they could send it up in the cable car because how did you build the cable car? It was a chicken and egg question that I sort of knew the answer to but it still made me gawp in amazement.

Big Ben stood up with a yawn and a stretch. 'Looks like this is us,' he said giving Bull a pat on the head. 'I sure hope they have someone there to help with the luggage.'

The cable car came into the upper station and in contrast to most cable cars that are in perpetual motion so just swing around the upper drum and go back down, this one came off the reel at the very top and onto a siding so we could unload our belongings. There were men waiting.

A series of bonjours were exchanged in the frigid air at the top of the mountain, then they set about loading our gear into a trailer on the back of a mini-van looking vehicle mounted on caterpillar tracks. It was wide and squat and had room for a family in the back. It was also warm. Far warmer than the cable car had been.

The cable car station was positioned at the leading edge of the resort. Directly in front of us were the two hotels. The Constantine on the left facing off against the Imperial on the right. Beyond them I could see restaurants, the sign for a pharmacy and shops selling and renting ski gear. There would be other businesses as well no doubt. It was quiet out, hardly any people visible in the resort. I pulled back the cuff on my coat to find my watch: it was 0708hrs which explained why the resort guests were not visible. I doubted I would be up this early again during my stay unless the case dictated I must. Soon the place would be teeming with tourists in bright ski-gear, all bustling about, and there would most likely be music piped over the raised speakers I could see. The street would be filled with the smells of food being cooked to lure hungry guests into restaurants and I realised I was reminiscing about just how wonderful ski-resorts could be. Wistfully, I once again wished Amanda could have come with me, it would have been a joy to have shared this with her. Not that Big Ben wasn't a great friend to go on adventures with, but if I am honest, he doesn't have boobs and that makes a lot of difference.

Our hotel was the one to our right, the caterpillar van taking us into an underground car park to demonstrate that the builders had thought of everything; guests could be unloaded out of the snow which must fall for a good portion of the year this high up.

Two different men were on hand to help us unload and carry the bags and ski gear inside, it truly was a five-star resort, which was demonstrated most keenly by everyone speaking English. If you have never been to France, or do not know the French then I will tell you this: they are a proud and noble nation and they like to speak their own language. Learn their language and they will welcome you, struggle to form a coherent sentence in French and they will leave you floundering. I am generalising of course, but the rules seemed to be different here.

A door opened ahead of us to reveal a huge bear of a man with a thick but well-trimmed beard. I recognised him instantly from the hotel's website. It was the owner and my client, Hubert Caron.

He raised a meaty hand in greeting. 'Good morning, gentlemen. Thank you for getting here so quickly.'

I crossed the few feet that separated us to shake his hand. 'Good morning, Monsieur. This is my colleague Ben Winters.' Hubert had a very strong grip and a right hand so huge mine felt swamped by it.

'Come in out of the cold, boys. You'll have plenty of time to be cold later while you look for our Yeti.' He indicated with his head that we should follow. 'Don't worry about your bags. I will have everything taken up to your rooms.' I followed him through a door, the dogs pulling against their leads to get inside first as always.

It hadn't been cold in the carpark bit, but I guess it hadn't been warm either, so the blast of heat inside was a wonderful change of pace. Big Ben and I immediately began stripping off layers.

At a wide, wooden reception desk that had been hewn from a single piece of timber, Hubert stopped and turned to us. 'I can have refreshments sent to your rooms if you are tired or would you like to press on with your investigation?

I noted that his question had been cleverly posed so that he was more likely to get us working straight away. Any other response would be an admission of weakness on our part. *Tired, ha! Tired is for civilians.* What I said was, 'I would like to discuss the case first. My colleague and I will then define our strategy and get our investigation under way.'

With a nod, he said, 'Very good,' and led us through to a small but well-appointed office where another man was waiting. 'Gentlemen, this is Police Chief Francois Delacroix.' The police chief was in uniform, not that it fit him very well. He appeared to be close to retirement and was certainly well into his sixties. His belly was a round ball of fat that sat on top of his belt as if held up by it and his face, like that of my client, had a weathered look I associated with spending a great deal of time outdoors in a harsh environment. I detected a scent of pipe smoke in the room and saw a pipe sitting in an ashtray on the coffee table in front of the chief. He stood up as we came into the room, advancing so he could shake our hands.

'Francois Delacroix at your service.' Yet again his English was impeccable. 'I'm afraid this investigation is beyond my meagre means.'

Hubert picked up the narrative. 'The police chief is the only police officer we have. He is supported by a larger department in Tignes, but they have classed my daughter's death as misadventure and thus there is to be no investigation.'

As he talked, he invited us to sit at one of a pair of sofas arranged around a coffee table. As we nestled into the small space, it was my turn

26

to speak, 'Mr Caron, please tell me when the Yeti was first seen and by whom.'

The police chief then reached into his pocket, producing an old white envelope that had faded with age. He began speaking, 'The Yeti was first seen in this area more than one hundred years ago.' He pulled some grainy black and white photographs from the envelope and spread them out on the desk while he continued talking. 'What you see here are the result of attacks and the remains of animals found slaughtered.'

The black and white photos were quite graphic in that the blood on the snow avoided all shades of grey to make a direct contrast between black and white. In one picture, it showed men standing around an indiscernible carcass that might have been an elk or a deer of some kind. In another, there was no carcass, but a blood trail leading through the snow and into the trees where it disappeared from sight. The next contained a man in police uniform holding a measure against a footprint. The footprint itself wasn't defined but one could still tell that it wasn't the print of any creature I recognised, and it was twice the size of a print that I would leave. It reminded me of a recent case where a sasquatch had been roaming the countryside near my house. The man inside the suit on that occasion had been not far short of seven feet tall, but the print he used as evidence of the beast had been artificially made. What none of the pictures contained was an image of the Yeti.

How convenient.

'Have there been human victims before this week?' I asked Hubert, keeping my voice quiet and respectful since the recent victim was the man's daughter.

He shook his head rather than speak, and it was the police chief that answered my question. 'Only one. In 1923, a man was killed on the west slope of Mt Chevale. He was reported missing by his wife. The man was a local business owner and was presumed dead when the villagers were unable to find him that first night. It was too cold for him to have survived, but it took three days to find his half eaten remains.'

Bull and Dozer were exploring the room. I had let them off their leads rather than put them on my lap as it is hard to conduct a serious conversation with a stupid sausage dog snoring upside down on your legs. At that moment Dozer popped his paws onto the coffee table to see if there was anything interesting on it. Hubert smiled. 'They will be popular here; my wife has a pair of long-haired girls.' He seemed greatly saddened by his daughter's death but was holding himself together.

I needed to ask him questions about the death though. 'Mr Caron, I need as much detail about the attack as possible.'

The grieving father shifted slightly in his chair, crossed his legs and inspected his fingers for a second before he started talking. We soon learned that his daughter had been skiing with a friend, a girl called Priscille Peran, two days ago. This was not unusual, she skied four or five times a week, but the other girl was someone that had arrived recently, a friend from her finishing school that had fallen on hard times and found employment at the rival hotel across the street. He had first learned of the accident when the police chief had called him late on Monday afternoon. Priscille had flagged down some other skiers after emerging from the woods with blood covering her face. She reported that they had been exploring off piste, heading for a slope his daughter believed would have fresh powder after the recent fall of snow, when a huge, horned, bipedal beast had attacked them. It wasn't the first time it had been seen. There had been twelve other reported sightings in the last three weeks, but all from a distance and no one had yet captured a picture. Priscille claimed to have been struck across the face when the beast attacked.

Knocked unconscious, she woke some time later to find Marie missing but a boot still containing her right foot was on the snow next to her.

With the sun beginning to set and temperature set to plummet, Chief Delacriox had formed a search party and scoured the area until Marie's body was found. He refused to describe the condition it was in, but Hubert spoke up instead, telling us that his daughter's head was missing. She had been decapitated and it had been his distraught wife that had identified her little girl's body from birth marks on her skin.

That was thirty-six hours ago.

I said, 'I need to see where she was killed.' Despite the sleep in Big Ben's car, I was still tired and Big Ben must be more so, but I was also energised now. This was a murder and I was going to prove it.

As we all stood up to leave, Hubert said, 'The hotel manager Michel Masson will be at your disposal throughout your stay.' He lifted the phone on his desk and pressed a single button. We waited as it connected, then listened as he spoke a few words in French and replaced it in its holder, 'Michel will be with you momentarily. I'm afraid I have to defer to my hotel's number one employee this week. I have my daughter's funeral to arrange, but Michel will be only too pleased to see to all of your needs.'

Next to me Big Ben, made a small squeak of excitement that I hoped no one else heard. Ignoring him, I nodded in acceptance then asked one more question before I left. 'Gentlemen, I have to ask if you believe there truly is a Yeti here? I ask because I expect there to be a person in a costume behind this and I need to know what would motivate them to target your daughter.' The question was designed to test their reaction, to see how deeply ingrained the Yeti legend was in these parts.

The two men exchanged a glance. 'You are very perceptive,' Hubert replied. 'I believe my rival, that pig Chevalier is to blame. He has been trying to put me out of business for years. Ever since he bought the hotel from the previous owner.' His voice was instantly filled with venom.

'Now then, Hubert, you have no evidence to support your accusations,' chided the police chief. 'If Monsieur Chevalier were guilty of anything, I would have caught him by now.'

'What are you referring to, please?' I asked.

Hubert grumpily rested a cheek on the edge of his desk. 'Gerard Chevalier has employed all manner of dirty tricks to damage my business. I never had any trouble with the previous owner, but ever since he took over, my hotel has suffered broken equipment, our water supply has been cut off three times, we had to shut once because a rat was found in our kitchen and I know he placed it there. I could kill the man.'

'Now then, Hubert. I can't have that kind of talk from you, especially since I have been turning a blind eye to the petty crimes I know *you* have been perpetrating against him in retaliation.'

Hubert swore in French and made a harrumph sound in response but had nothing further to say on the matter.

Deciding they were done, I asked another question, 'Where will I be able to find Priscille Peran, please? I should like to hear her account first hand.'

Just then there was a knock at the door, which opened inwards when Hubert called out, 'Come.' The person on the other side was a man dressed like a business man in a tailored suit, his eyes wide behind round glasses.

Big Ben huffed out his breath and made a disgruntled sound; Michel was a man's name in France.

30

The hotel manager was perhaps forty years old, but his hands were bereft of a ring which I took to mean he was either unmarried or long divorced but he looked young, his complexion near perfect like a schoolboy's. Only his hair, which had a few wisps of grey provided a hint at his true age. 'Ah, Michel.' He turned his attention to me, 'Michel will be able to furnish you with all the information you may need.' Then he swung his gaze back to his hotel manager as he said, 'These are the two gentlemen I told you about. Please give them everything they want.'

We were about to leave, so I turned to shake the client's hand as was my custom. 'Monsieur Caron I cannot promise a swift conclusion; however, I can assure you this will have my undivided attention until I am able to identify your daughter's killer.'

His meaty hand closed around mine again as he pumped my arm. 'I wish you luck. This is damaging my business more even than the unwarranted attempts of that fool across the road. I hope for a speedy conclusion.'

The police chief took that as his cue to leave, Michel backing out of the door to make room for him. Big Ben and I followed him out to find Michel waiting for us. We followed him back to reception, the two dogs sniffing along happily at my feet. There we all stopped again as he came to a halt and turned to face us.

He hit me with a professionally warm smile. 'Your friend Jajj... Jaggit?'

'Jagjit,' I supplied.

'Oui, Jagjit. He told me about a man who has no fear. A man who faces down evil creatures with a steel rod where his spine ought to be. He didn't mention you were so handsome though.' I considered blushing and struggled to come up with an appropriate response. I didn't need to though because now he was looking at Big Ben. 'And he said no harm could ever come to the man because he has a friend who is indestructible.' His French accent was forming the words in the most sensuously sultry voice he could muster, and he was staring up at Big Ben in a way that made me think he wanted to cover him in toffee sauce and eat him with a spoon. He was gay and clearly hoped we were too.

He cocked a hip to one side as he ran his eyes up and down him. 'Tell me, how much can you bench press? I bet it is an impressive number.'

'It's about four of you,' Big Ben replied, his voice as neutral as he could manage. Like me, Big Ben was on a strictly no sausage diet when it came to relationships but though neither of us was even remotely homophobic, we were also not about to experiment either.

Michel was all but panting as he said, 'I know you have work to do, but when you are done catching the Yeti, I may have a few tasks for you to perform.' He wasn't picking up on the obvious cues Big Ben was putting out. Then he stepped inside Big Ben's personal space, clasping his arms behind his back as he did which made him look more vulnerable. 'Don't worry,' he smouldered up at him, 'I don't bite. It's not like I have a safety word.' He leaned in closer to whisper loudly enough for me to hear, 'It's tangerine.'

Wowza. This guy was a bit full-on. There certainly wasn't much grey area about his intentions. I took a step back from him. 'Look, I'll, ah. I'll sort the dogs out and unpack. I need a Ski-Doo if you can arrange one and a map and I need a number where I can reach Priscille Peran, the lady that was injured in the attack on Monday.' I gave Big Ben a slap on the shoulder, 'Catch up later?' I said with a wink.

'Where are you going?' Michel asked. 'I want both of you. Per'aps you would be so kind as to Eiffel Tower me later.'

I couldn't help my eyes brows shooting to the top of my forehead. If they had gone any faster, they might have kept going and fallen to the floor behind me. 'Eiffel Tower you? What's that?' I asked genuinely mystified.

Big Ben said, 'It's…ah. I'll draw you a picture later, okay?'

'Yeah sure,' I replied, not altogether sure I wanted to see the picture.

'You are sweet, Tempest Michaels,' Michel reached up to trace a finger along my collar bone and I took a step back to avoid being touched as I was getting a little weirded out by his overt intentions. He said, 'Sweet and innocent. I will enjoy… educating you.' His pupils were dilated to saucers as he stared into mine.

'I think I'll pass, but my big friend here ought to be able to satisfy your needs.'

Big Ben punched me on the shoulder. Hard.

'Sorry, old boy,' he said to Michel, 'I'm strictly girls only.'

Michel looked surprised but replied with, 'You gentlemen will not be the first to change their minds. We shall 'ave such fun together.'

'O-okay,' was all I could manage in response. 'Michel, our things were taken to our rooms, but we were not given room keys or even numbers.'

He gathered himself, recovering quickly from Big Ben's snubbing, 'Please come with me, gentlemen.' At the reception desk, he spoke in French to the lady behind the counter who produced two keys and then instructed us on where to find our rooms. 'I will have a pair of Ski-Doos at your disposal throughout your stay and will make contact with Mademoiselle Peran. She is a member of staff at the Imperial but will not be working I am certain. Will there be anything else?'

33

'I need to speak with Mrs Caron.' The hotel manager sucked in his breath. I continued, 'Mrs Caron identified her daughter's body, it is unfortunate, but I will need to speak with her if I am to investigate this case.'

'Very well, Monsieur. I will pass the message. Anything else.'

One final question occurred, 'My friend Jagjit and his wife, where can I find them?'

He turned slightly to speak again with the lady behind reception. The answer came in French and though my ability stopped at school and was quite limited, I understood the answer: They were in the Honeymoon suite. Good for them.

To Big Ben I said, 'Time to go to work.'

I had a stack of questions for him but as we walked away it was he that asked the first one, 'Did you notice that the client is more concerned about the prosperity of his hotel than the death of his daughter?'

I nodded grimly, 'He barely seems upset at all.'

'So, what's the plan? See if we can get to the injured woman this morning and if not arrange to meet her later and set off to see the scene of the attack?'

'That is exactly the plan,' I replied. 'With a brief hiatus where we get a shower and some food and a change of clothes. I need to feed the dogs and make sure they do their business before we head out too. Are you not tired?'

'Not desperately. It's day time now so I will probably do better to push through and get an early night,' he replied. I had to acknowledge that he didn't look tired. He needed a shave, we both did but in such a frigid atmosphere, I would be letting my whiskers grow instead.

His mention of an early night prompted another question though, 'Ben, I have to ask what just went on with the hotel manager. Are we throwing off gay vibes today? Do I need to change my aftershave?'

He turned to me with a quizzical expression. 'Really? You couldn't tell? He's involved mate. That little display was to throw us both off guard and distract us from what he is up to.'

I thought about that for a second. Big Ben might be onto something. We had made it upstairs to our floor, the dogs pulling hard at their leads to get to wherever it was we were going, so I was reading off room numbers as I looked for the one that matched the key in my hand. 'Ah, here we are,' I said. Our doors were side by side in a wide corridor tastefully fitted out with wood panelling on the walls and wooden floor boards beneath our feet. On the walls in the corridor were large black and white photographs of skiers across the decades, many of them sporting what would have been early equipment that must have been heavy and cumbersome to wear and use. The pioneers; how people fail to appreciate them.

Big Ben's voice brought me back to the now. 'Obviously I am used to men throwing themselves at me. It is a daily occurrence, and a consequence of being this damned handsome.' I rolled my eyes. 'There is an ulterior motive though. He was trying to distract us, and he might not even be gay. We will have to watch him and find out what his connection to the daughter was.'

I could present no argument and had not yet formed the same conclusion he had. I tapped my watch. 'Rendezvous for breakfast in thirty?'

'Roger.' We both pushed our doors open and went inside.

My suitcase and other belongings had been stacked in my room. My skis were in a compartment for them by the door along with my poles and helmet. The room itself was bigger than I had expected, commanding a view over the ski slopes and mountains of Val-d'Isère beyond. The rooms had been arranged by Hubert as part of my expenses, but I had to wonder what the standard peak season price was.

The dogs were hovering around my feet, waiting for me to unpack their bed. I wanted a shower and to clean my teeth, but their needs had to come first and the one thing I wanted to ensure I covered was their bathroom needs. Let me tell you though, my dogs aren't as dumb as one might think. I took out their onesies again and they both hid under the bed.

I couldn't tell whether they disapproved of the fashion or correlated putting the garment on with going back out in the cold, but they wanted none of it. Having learned long ago that positive reinforcement worked better than negative chastisement, I took out the box of gravy bones I had brought with me.

'I'll bet you'll do it for a scooby snack,' I coaxed, laying on my front to peer under the bed.

Had they been able to articulate a response it might have been, 'No thanks. We'll just pick a corner to pee in.'

'Come out, boys, come on. It won't take long if you just get on with it.'

As you might imagine, five minutes later they were outside turning the snow yellow around the corner from the hotel, but not until my coaxing had become impatient demands and eventually a frustrated use of a ski to lever them from their hiding place.

Bull especially was eyeing me with an expression that might need to be bleeped out if it could be translated. I supplied them with another gravy bone for their efforts when we got back to the room and arranged their bed beneath a radiator so they could burrow and sleep and be ridiculously hot the way Dachshunds prefer.

Finally, with their needs attended to, I was able to strip off and deal with my own scuzziness. I was hoping to find Jagjit and Alice at breakfast but hadn't called their room as, well, they are newlyweds and might be awake but still in bed. I'm sure you can join the dots. In the shower, I ran through what I already knew.

A woman had been killed on the slopes and another woman injured. This meant I had an eyewitness that could tell me more about what she had seen. That she had reported being attacked by a Yeti made her testimony dubious at best but I didn't want to judge too quickly, maybe she had been attacked from behind. The client came across as more upset by the potential impact to his business than the loss of his daughter and I needed to meet his wife, the dead woman's mother, and speak with her since she had identified the body. That might be a tricky and unpleasant conversation. Back in the army, it had fallen to me on a few occasions to deliver the terrible news of a soldier's death to a mother or a wife. Witnessing the distress, disbelief and subsequent inability to process the news had stayed with me as much as witnessing the deaths first hand myself. I wondered what Mrs Caron's emotional state would be like. Finally, the client had accused his rival hotel owner across the street of his daughter's murder so at least he wasn't buying the idea that there was a real Yeti though the police chief seemed to prefer the less rational explanation.

As I dried my skin and dug out the long socks and other clothing bought specifically for skiing, I felt the familiar pull of the mystery beckoning.

The dogs came with me to the restaurant for breakfast. Unlike in England, dogs are welcome almost everywhere in many European countries and can be found under tables in restaurants all the time. I would feed them a few morsels as a peace offering for forcing them out in the cold.

Looking around for Big Ben as I came into the room, I spotted instead, a very familiar Indian chap and his lovely wife. They were across the room at a table set for four, holding hands and drinking coffee. I paused for a minute, questioning whether I was invading a private moment.

Then from behind me, I heard, 'Oi, shagfesters. Come up for air, have you?' Big Ben didn't come loaded with the same sensitivity as other humans. Every head in the place turned to look at him, at which point he indicated to the staring faces that the shout had come from me. I refused to let my face colour as a hundred or more eyes questioned why I felt the need to be so loud.

Alice had seen us, of course, and waved as Jagjit, with his back to us, had to turn around to do the same. He let go his wife's hand and stood up as we approached. 'Hey, guys. That didn't take you long. When did you arrive?'

Big Ben didn't pause long at Jagjit's table though, he was hungry and heading for the huge breakfast buffet of food on offer. 'Mmmm, coffee,' he said as he went by me. I echoed his sentiment, saying that I would be back once I had visited the coffee pot and followed Big Ben. By the time I got there, he had a pain au chocolat in his mouth and two more on a plate plus a mug of coffee in his right hand. Quite how he managed to stay lean when he ate so much garbage I would never fathom.

I loaded my plate with fruit and natural yoghurt, filled a mug with dark, unctuous coffee and followed Big Ben back to the table and our friends. There was a brief bout of handshaking and air kissing in Alice's case as we settled down.

'Hilary and Anthea will be along in a minute,' said Jagjit. I thought I had misheard him for a moment. 'They arrived last night,' Jagjit explained to my confused expression. 'They flew in. Didn't you know they were coming?'

I shook my head and swallowed my mouthful of breakfast. 'Hilary never mentioned it. Are their kids here?'

'They dropped them off with Anthea's parents,' supplied Alice. 'I think it was a spur of the moment thing.'

Big Ben looked up from the plate of food he was devouring, to point across the room. 'Here they come now.'

I turned to see where he was pointing, then stood as yet another friend was joining us. Hilary was a top chap and had recently saved my life, so I felt a general warmth towards him. However, his wife Anthea and I had a difficult relationship which was entirely because she had decided at some point in the past that she didn't like me. She had cooled a little, but only a little, though I wasn't going to let that spoil the mood.

'Hi, guys,' I greeted them as they wove their way across the room. 'I had no idea you had decided to come as well. Are you just here for a vacation?'

Hilary shook my hand and slapped me on the shoulder. 'It was a spontaneous thing. We haven't been skiing since the kids came along and it seemed like a perfect opportunity.'

'I said you would just get killed without my Brian here to help,' supplied Anthea in a less than pleasant tone. 'That witch would have done the job if it hadn't been for him.'

'She most certainly would have,' I agreed. I was quite certain she didn't need to keep pointing out my debt to him, but I smiled and turned my attention back to her husband. 'How's the shoulder?' During the battle with the witch, when he came to my rescue just as she was about to electrocute me, he had turned the weapon on her but had dislocated his arm in the process.

'Much better,' he said. 'Now, I need some breakfast. I'm starving.'

Over breakfast we discussed everyone's plan for the day. My plan was to go to the Imperial Hotel to visit Priscille. I didn't have an appointment but I did have time so I was going to ask to see her and wait until she appeared. Big Ben would get a couple of hours sleep. The other four were going skiing, the threat of a Yeti insufficient to worry them. It hadn't been seen on the pistes after all. However, when I mentioned that Big Ben and I intended to take Ski-Doos to the attack site, Jagjit and Hilary both wanted to come along. The ladies had no such interest so would be found in the spa they said.

With breakfast finished and feeling suitably full, we split up and went our separate ways. Big Ben was going to check with the police chief as we needed him to show us the attack site and make sure the hotel could provide another two Ski-Doos for Jagjit and Hilary. The loose plan was to head up the mountain after lunch. It was later than I intended but gave the two couples a morning on the slopes. I could busy myself snooping around in the resort until it was time to go.

As the others departed, I ran through a mental checklist, decided I had all I needed and took the dogs to find the injured Priscille.

I had to wait in the reception of the Imperial Hotel while Priscille was located. I was expected, the man at the reception desk said, and she would be with me shortly. Michel had done as promised and passed a message that I wished to speak with her. Sitting in a large leather chair, I scanned around the area I was in. The Imperial Hotel was larger and more expensively decorated than my client's. To my untrained eye, it appeared as if no expense had been spared when they decorated the place. Perhaps, the superior nature of the hotel was one of the reasons my client was so opposed to it. Hubert claimed his business was negatively affected but there had been a crowd at breakfast this morning, so I had to question by what percentage his revenue was down.

I had waited just long enough to begin getting bored, when a tall, well-dressed man that had been speaking with the chap on the reception desk came my way. It was clear he was coming to speak with me as there was no one else near me. I rose to greet him, but Dozer and Bull took a dislike to the man and began barking.

They were lunging at his legs, the man's face showing surprise at their ferocity which then turned to laughter. Thankfully, they were still on their leads and couldn't get to him, but as he chuckled at my dogs, I considered letting them go.

'They are so funny,' he said looking at them rather than me. I fixed my face, so I wasn't squinting a narrow expression when he looked back up. 'Gils Chevalier,' he introduced himself finally, the name combined with his age telling me he was the Imperial Hotel owner's son.

I gripped his hand in mine as I replied, 'Tempest Michaels.'

'Yes. You're here to see Priscille. I'm afraid she is very delicate still so this will have to be a short meeting. The attack rattled her emotional state and the injury to her face is... well, she is, was young and pretty and has been in hiding ever since. We are trying to look after her, of course. As her employers, we are paying for whatever plastic surgery they can perform to repair her face. For today though, please keep your questions limited to the attack itself. I will be joining you to ensure you do not upset her.' He leaned forward to get into my face as he delivered the last sentence as a quiet threat. He was being very protective of the girl, unnecessarily I felt, but instead of reacting I chose to assume that there had been other persons that had upset her in their bid to speak with her already.

'Lead on,' I replied neutrally.

As he straightened, turned and walked away, I followed behind. The son of my client's rival hotel owner was taller even than Big Ben by my estimation. Not by much, but men of that height were rare. He was also very good looking with flowing brown hair pulled into a man-bun on top of his head and a short but trim beard. He made the effect look effortless, but it was working for him. I judged his age to be somewhere around thirty and was willing to bet that his looks combined with the family money made him an attractive proposition for the visiting ladies.

He took me through a door and into a room that had a view over a slope that swept down to a ski-lift in the distance. Skiers were already whizzing by outside. There were logs burning in a stone fireplace to my left where several chairs had been arranged. Sitting in the one furthest from the fire was a petite woman, her feet tucked around and beneath her bottom as she held her hands out to warm them. Her head was a swathe of bandages that covered her whole scalp save for a few tufts of hair poking out where the bandages had moved. The dressing covered all of the left-hand side of her face and looped beneath her chin to keep it in

44

place. Her eyes were hidden behind wide-lensed sunglasses. It wasn't bright in the room so they had to be to hide blackeyes from the attack.

The dogs were pulling at their leads, trying desperately to cross the room and see the lady who they were certain would shower them both with attention. That she was sat next to an open fire they could warm their bellies against just added to the prize if they could just break free. I did my best to keep them under control.

'Priscille, this is Tempest Michaels, the detective I told you about,' Gils said as he knelt next to her and took her hand.

It was a gesture that suggested a level of intimacy beyond the usual employer/employee. Maybe I was reading too much into it and I decided to keep quiet as he rose again and offered me the seat nearest the fireplace. The dogs fussed about Priscille's chair until she patted them idly a few times. It was enough to settle them, so as she looked back up at me, the two dogs curled into balls and went to sleep in front of the flames.

I offered the young woman my hand which she shook limply. 'How can I 'elp you, Monsieur Michaels,' she asked, her French accent thicker than others I had heard today.

'Thank you for speaking with me, Priscille. I am here to find out who attacked you.'

'Who?' she interrupted me. 'Surely, you mean what. It was a Yeti,' she stated.

I tilted my head to one side. 'I thought you didn't see the creature.'

The one cheek that was showing coloured slightly, but she regained control quickly. 'I didn't, but something tore my friend's head off and left me with disfiguring injuries. It wasn't a man that did that.'

I moved on. 'Can you tell me what happened. How it was that you came to be where you were and the events after you regained consciousness.'

Priscille nodded her head as she launched into a well-practiced story; no doubt she had told it many times now. I made notes as she spoke, assuming that she would embellish some parts like everyone else does, but the story sounded exactly like the one I had heard this morning from the client and the police chief. The girls were both experienced skiers that regularly left the pistes as they sought fresh snow and adventurous routes. I learned that Priscille had met Marie Caron at a finishing school in Paris. Their families were of equal standing, but a few months ago and just weeks before graduating, Priscille's father committed suicide and it was revealed that he had made several poor business decisions and squandered his fortune as he tried to gamble his way out of debt. Her mother had died some years before that which left Priscille destitute and without family. The poor woman told the story while staring into the fire with an emotionless face.

Her friend Marie had come to the rescue, providing a job and a place to live through her good friend Gils. If I chose to believe Priscille, Marie had tried to secure her a role at her father's hotel first, only to be refused. She almost spat Hubert's name when she said it. Gils though, had been accommodating. I made a mental note about the way she had looked at him when she said his name.

The two girls had taken a path through the woods which they knew would lead them to a narrow slope known only to locals. Its obscurity meant they could expect untouched powder after the recent fall of snow, but it was there in the woods that the Yeti had attacked. Priscille said that it hit her from behind and confirmed that she had not seen it for herself, but had awoken covered in blood to find another blood trail leading away from a boot that still contained Marie's left foot. She struggled speaking at this point, Gils finding a tissue to offer her before I could.

'Would you like me to come back?' I asked.

She shook her head and sniffed before loudly blowing her nose. 'There is not much more to tell, Monsieur Michaels. I couldn't find Marie and I was so dizzy. I stumbled through the woods worried that the sun would set before I found anyone else. I would surely have frozen to death if I hadn't made it back to the piste before it closed for the day.' She talked a little about her injuries, crying a little as she complained about how difficult it had been to see her own exposed cheekbone and how lucky she was to still have both her eyes.

I could find nothing to say. I had seen facial injuries before: the person never truly heals.

It was Gils that came to my rescue, breaking the silence when he asked, 'What will you do now, Mr Michaels?'

I took a moment to stare at my notes. So far, I hadn't revealed anything that felt like a clue. Someone had attacked and killed one girl and injured another. There would be a reason behind that, just as there would be a reason why they thought pretending to be a Yeti was a good idea. The Yeti costume was most likely to throw blame on a mythical creature that would now vanish in the hope that the trail would go cold. They were waiting for an answer though, so I gave them one.

'In my time as a paranormal investigator, I have yet to come across anything even remotely mysterious. This case will be the same, I'm afraid. The Yeti is a man in a costume. The footprints in the snow have been artificially made and there will be a reason for Marie's murder.' Gils and Priscille shared a look that could have meant anything. 'I will find the reason behind her murder and catch the killer.' I delivered the statement in a determined voice which caused their gazes to swing to me. 'It's what I do,' I finished.

'You believe this to be the work of a man and that Marie was murdered?' asked Gils.

I nodded. 'I do.'

'Why would anyone want to hurt Marie?' asked Priscille.

'That is precisely what I intend to find out,' I replied as I quietly closed my notebook.

Priscille hadn't finished though. 'She was so sweet, such a lovely and generous girl. She was loved here. By everyone but her father that is.'

I just about managed to not react to her statement. I did ask her to clarify what she had said though. 'Priscille, what do you mean by that?'

She tutted at herself as if she hadn't meant to reveal so much, then sighed but started talking anyway, 'Hubert Caron is a pig. He thought he could control every element of his daughter's life. Where she went to school, who her friends were, who she could fall in love with. If you are looking for a killer, you should look at your client first.'

It was quite the bold statement. 'Who was she in love with?' I asked. It felt like something that could be pertinent to know.

Priscille pursed her lips. 'I am not willing to tell you that, Monsieur Michaels.'

I considered pressing her for an answer, but it didn't feel like the right time to do so, and I wondered if her reluctance to answer, and Hubert's interference, were because Marie had been in love with Priscille.

I didn't voice my thought though. There seemed no advantage in discussing the subject at this juncture. I rose to my feet and shook her hand lightly again. Gils stood also, so he could show me out.

I had one question for Gils before I went. 'Gils, my client...'

'Hubert Caron,' he supplied.

'Yes, Monsieur Caron...'

'May our prayers be with his family at this terrible time,' he interrupted again.

I pressed on. 'He expressed a rivalry between his hotel and yours and suggested a policy of dirty tricks had been perpetrated against his hotel. How deep does the... dislike go?' I asked.

If the question surprised Gils, he showed no sign. 'My father and Monsieur Caron have been enemies for years but I believe that the petty crimes Hubert accuses my father of started because of an accident. I must ask: is it your task here to prove that my father is responsible for Marie Caron's death?'

'Not at all. I was hired to catch the Yeti. There won't be one of course, just a man in a suit fitted with oversize feet. I am going up the mountain now to see the attack site.'

'You're going out there to look for the Yeti?' Priscille asked, her voice filled with incredulity.

I nodded. 'The police chief is taking me. I doubt I can solve this thing from my hotel room.'

Gils said, 'Good luck, Mr Michaels,' as he escorted to me to the door, his long arm out to guide me. I was going anyway, my dogs reluctantly trotting along behind as I tugged them away from the warm fireplace.

There was something odd about Priscille and Gils. Maybe they were sleeping together and it was nothing more than that. I filed it away for later and went back out into the cold.

Despite telling myself that this wasn't meant to be a holiday, I was loving the resort and couldn't wait to solve the case so I could have a few days skiing. The trip up the mountain to the site of the attack was planned for as soon as I was available, and the other chaps had returned from their morning ski. It was nearing lunchtime, so the obvious plan was to head out after that, take the Ski-Doos because it gave us easy manoeuvrability and see what there was to see. There might be nothing, but I wouldn't find out by staying in the nice warm hotel.

As I neared my room, the door of the room next to mine opened and a man came out, shutting the door behind him.

I said, 'Bonjour,' as we passed each other since it was the polite thing to do.

He replied but it was clear from his accent that he was not French. I couldn't say where he did come from though, maybe a Russian state I thought, but hard to tell with one accent affecting a language I wasn't all that familiar with. It carried no importance, so I forgot it immediately as I went through my own door and started thinking about calling Amanda.

I checked my watch: 1143hrs. It was an hour earlier in the UK but she would either be at the office or involved in the case she had been trying to sew up. Big Ben was probably getting a little sleep so I would rouse him in time for lunch and give Amanda a call now.

She answered almost before it had rung. 'Hi, Tempest, how's the snow?' she asked.

I couldn't help smiling at the sound of her voice. 'Hey, babe. The snow is cold. The dogs don't like it. How's the case going?'

'Actually, I just closed it. I'm all wrapped up at this end, so... is the offer of a date in France still on?'

My pulse instantly tapped out a fast staccato at the thought of having her staying in the fabulous hotel with me. Suddenly feeling warm and ignoring the voice coming from my pants, I said, 'Absolutely, Amanda. How soon can you get here?'

'There's a flight to Chambéry at teatime. If I'm quick I can make it.'

'Won't that get you here really late?' I asked. Chambéry wasn't exactly around the corner.

'I have to get a train into Tignes and then transfer to a coach and then get the cable car up the mountain, but there is a single-ticket service because they want people to get to the ski resorts in the area. It should get me there by ten o'clock.' I cringed as she said the time. Amanda steadfastly refused to use a twenty-four-hour clock just because it annoyed me. It was our first cute couple thing, although I would never call it that openly.

I couldn't hide my excitement though. 'That sounds wonderful,' I murmured in a husky voice as I thought about the possibilities her joining me here presented. Then I caught myself, and asked, 'Do you want me to book you a room?'

At the other end of the line, she returned a snigger. 'No, Tempest. We are both adults, I think we can share a room.' My heart was really hammering in my chest now. 'Besides,' she purred in a sultry voice, 'I know I can rely on you to be a complete gentleman.'

I almost choked and the sound it made was audible because Amanda burst out laughing. She was teasing me. 'I'm sorry, Tempest. You are such an easy mark. Look, I'll be there in a few hours and I expect to be pampered when I arrive so go make preparations.'

'Yes, ma'am,' I replied.

'Good boy. Heck, I need to go pack. I'll text you en route.'

Bull nudged my foot for a pick up. I was sitting on the edge of the bed and it was too high for him to climb on to. I lifted him and then his brother so they could settle down for an afternoon of sleep while I was out. 'Enjoy the bed, chaps. I don't think you will get to be back in here much this week.' With that enticing thought reverberating inside my head I pulled the footstool from the dressing table across to the bed to make a step so they could get off and back on if they needed a drink. Then, with half an hour to kill, I read through my notes, sent a message to Jane back at the office telling her to have a couple of easy days while Amanda and I were both away, and wondered to myself what it might be that was motivating the daft, fake Yeti attacks.

It was 1230hrs soon enough, my phone beeping with a text from Big Ben asking if I was ready for lunch before I could text him the same question. We met outside in the corridor, the dogs staying in my room and looking quite content to do so.

'Good sleep?' I asked.

'I was alone, so... no. I tell you, Tempest, hanging out with you is having a very negative impact on my sex life. I should have been rolling in women by now. Tonight, you get to be wingman as I predate this resort and select some fine ladies to accompany me back to my hotel room.'

'Ah, yes, about that. Amanda is on her way here. I expect to be otherwise engaged tonight.'

'Really? This is turning into couples central. What the heck happened. A few weeks ago, only Hilary had a woman to drag him down. Now you are all at it.'

'Yeah, sorry about that. Good luck with the women tonight though.'

'Hah! Not that I need your help, but you owe me, and I am sure you can find a couple of hours to come out and see the magnificence.'

'Of the resort at night?' I asked confused at his sentence.

'Of Big Ben in full pants-wetting, throw your knickers in the air brilliance. I need a healthy dose of boobies. Like I said, you get to be my wingman. You can hold my pint while I impress them and you can act as a scale model so they can see what a normal man looks like in comparison to my magnificence.'

'Riiiight,' I drawled.

Listening to Big Ben's fluent rubbish had taken us all the way downstairs to the restaurant and bar area again. There were patrons in the restaurant ordering food and a few people at the bar already drinking despite the early hour, no doubt excusing themselves because they were on holiday.

We looked around for Jagjit and the others. 'They must still be on the snow,' Big Ben observed. 'They can find us, I'm hungry.' He slapped me on the shoulder and left me behind as he flagged down a waitress to organise a table for six.

I was hungry too, and quite content that our friends would appear soon enough and wouldn't mind that we had eaten without them. Looking around the hotel, there was no sense that a woman had been attacked and brutally killed by what people were reporting to be a monstrous beast. The guests were mostly dressed in ski clothing, the outer layers stripped off in deference to the warmth indoors. Would panic set in if the beast was seen again? Would it even make another appearance if the only reason for its existence was to kill Marie Caron? That the murderer had taken the costume and destroyed it or planned to never put it back on felt like a very real possibility. As I joined Big Ben at the table where he was now chatting up two young and quite lovely waitresses, I wondered if this case might prove to be tougher than I had first imagined.

Hurtling up the mountain on the gas-powered Ski-Doos was great fun. They flew over the snow as we sort of followed the police chief while also racing each other at the same time. If we had known where we were going, it would have been an all-out battle to get there. As it was, like boys, we kept picking the next spot to get to first. The machine was not one I had ever ridden before, but the controls were familiar, resembling those of a motorbike with a twist-grip throttle and handlebar brakes.

It was cold out, which might seem like an obvious statement, but the sun was beating down on us and would have been warm if the air had been still. Our passage through it at break-neck speed was creating the chill.

When we set off, Francois had warned of a storm approaching the region. It might veer away yet, but warnings were in place for heavy snow and high winds which this far up the mountain might be dangerous. Unfortunately for the police chief, whose intention had been to convince us to postpone I think, he instead provided an excuse for driving the Ski-Doos as fast as we could.

My lips were going numb from the cold, but I wasn't about to slow down as I was winning this particular heat. Ahead of me, the ski-lift support that Big Ben had picked out as the next target was getting close. I couldn't get the throttle to open any further and had lost every race so far because the other machines all went faster than mine, even the chief's probably though he had declined to join in the fun. This time I had gotten a head start by unashamedly cheating. Despite that, the chaps were now catching me. Hilary's machine was closest, bearing down on my right-hand side. He had made it to the marker first more than half the time and I wondered if he was just better at controlling his machine, if his machine was actually the fastest one or if, because he was the lightest, his machine was able to skip across the surface a little easier.

Whatever the case, I swerved to block his path, forcing him to alter his course and go around several trees he might otherwise have hit. The manoeuvre defeated Hilary but slowed my machine by just enough that Jagjit overhauled me to pip me at the post. It was all in good humour though.

The route had taken us up the piste that led back down to the hotels and the resort of Harvati. Skiers were whipping by to our right as we stuck to the left-hand edge of the trees that bordered the slope. We were stopped now at a junction where several slopes met as we waited for the Chief to catch up to us. He rumbled along a minute later, halting his machine perpendicular to ours.

'We turn off the piste just up there,' he pointed. 'It's not far now and we will have to go single file through the woods.'

I replied with, 'Roger,' a habit I probably needed to shake. He led off with the rest of us following in a snaking line of Ski-Doos. True to his word, we shortly took a left turn through the trees but continued on slowly for what felt like another twenty minutes before I spied yellow barrier tape through the trees.

The attack site wouldn't be found by accident, it was on no one's route to anywhere. The police chief brought his machine to a stop, killed the engine, and got off, stretching his body in place as if it had stiffened during the ride. The rest of us pulled up along the same trail but spread out wherever we came to a halt.

'It's just through here,' said Francois as he ducked under the barrier tape.

I didn't move, turning instead to face the guys, 'Chaps, that's an actual murder scene ahead. If you want to stay here and guard the Ski-Doos...'

'Sure,' said Hilary, 'I have no desire to see buckets of blood in the snow. It'll give me nightmares for weeks.'

Jagjit grimaced. 'Yeah, that sounds unappealing. I'll stay here too.'

Big Ben had already ducked the tape and was following the chief as he wound between the trees. I hurried to catch up, my feet sinking in the deep snow and branches catching my clothing. I reached them just as Francois stopped.

'This is it,' he said, indicating the general area with his hand. 'We found the foot over by that tree and the blood trail and footprints went off through the trees to the east until it reached the cliff edge about seventy metres from here.'

'What happened to it then?' Big Ben asked.

'It appears to go over the edge as if the creature climbed down, but we could find no trace of anything on the ground below, not even a drop of blood. The footprints just stop as if the creature learned to fly or indeed went over the edge but there are no caves for it to go into. The body was found about fifty metres to the north.' The police chief's tone was professionally removed. He was just doing his job, but I got the feeling that he had taken the job here because it was easy, and the worst crime he ever had to deal with was petty theft. Now he had a grisly death and too few ideas about what he was supposed to do next.

The blood was still visible in places, but fresh snow and drifting snow had covered most of it. Whatever footprints there had been were obscured now so all I had were the photographs he had shown me this morning.

'How far is the drop?' I asked.

Francois swung to face me. 'That's what we call the knife edge. It's a thousand metres straight down. Climbers kill themselves on it every year.'

I turned in place, looking about me and trying to visualise the scene. The attacker had to have charged them, knocking Priscille down and possibly inflicting her facial wound with the first blow. She hadn't been the target though and the killer was confident enough that he allowed her to live. The body had been torn apart, one foot and the head getting removed and since the head was still missing it made sense to me that the killer had stabbed or shot her in the head and then inflicted the wounds to resemble an animal attack.

It was a lot of effort, but if they got away with murder then maybe they had the right tactic. Looking about still, a question occurred to me, 'Francois, what were they doing here?'

He looked up surprised. 'They were going from the piste to the fresh powder that borders the knife edge. It's a bit too dangerous for most skiers and only the locals know about it, but Marie grew up here. The people I interviewed said she skied it all the time because no one else did.'

I looked about again, frowning. 'But where they were attacked doesn't link the piste to... anything. The track we parked the Ski-Doos on would be the obvious path to stick to. There's barely enough room to ski here and all kinds of branches in the way.' Something about where they had been attacked was wrong. If I wanted to reach this particular spot, I would ditch my skis and walk.

While I thought about that, I walked toward where Francois had said the foot was found. There was a dark stain at the base of a tree which was almost certainly Marie's blood. Then I spotted something moving in the light breeze. Snagged on a piece of bark was what looked like fur. It had been missed by the police and everyone else that had come to the site.

'Ben,' I called. He was a few feet away but answered and trudged through the snow to get to me. 'Can you cup your hands around this?'

'Err, sure. What is it?' he asked.

'A piece of fur.' When he squinted, he saw it too. 'It might be nothing and I need to get a proper look at it but it looks like artificial fur, the type you get in the collar of a coat. I don't want it to disappear on the wind when I tease it free though.'

He nodded his understanding and cupped his hands to shield it from the air while I produced an evidence bag from my pocket. Then, with bare hands despite the cold, I gently pulled the strands free.

Then a voice ripped through the air to grab our attention. Both Big Ben and I turned to see what was occurring.

With panicked faces, Jagjit and Hilary were running toward us evidently terrified about something behind them. Running though in the deep snow was proving quite difficult and they were part clawing, part swimming, part pulling themselves along by grabbing trees, but they were both shouting as loud as they could.

And what they were shouting was: 'YETI!'

The Yeti. Wednesday, November 30th 1502hrs

My first reaction was to chuckle. My good friends had been left alone and had managed to creep each other out. Now they had seen something and panicked. Or they were trying to play a trick on us.

I stepped forward to intercept them just as Big Ben was making a comment about crazy civilians but then I saw something moving through the trees behind them. I crouched to look. It was a good thirty yards behind them but definitely coming their way and it was big and white.

I stood up again glancing around for Big Ben. 'Ben.'

'Yeah?'

'It's show time.' I pointed to the man in the costume coming our way. My adrenalin was spiking but I was feeling victorious. The killer had somehow heard we were here and had come to scare us off. It was a ballsy move. What if we had weapons? This was our chance to wrap the case up though. The chief could cuff him, we could interview him back at the hotel and he could be taken away. Neat and tidy and all done in time for Amanda to arrive to spend a few days with me without distractions.

Now there was a warming thought.

'Shall we introduce ourselves?' Big Ben asked but he hadn't waited for my reply. He was already heading toward it.

I followed, soon catching up to him as he met with Jagjit and Hilary. They were red in the face and out of breath.

'It's a Yeti,' puffed Hilary. 'We came to warn you.'

I patted him on the shoulder. 'Get your breath, we've got this.' The shambling white lump was on all fours and heading our way still. The head was pointing toward us, two black eyes shining in our direction. It was a great costume. It even had twin horns from the top of its skull that curled like a ram's. I had no particular fear. Unless the man in the costume was armed, I doubted he stood any chance at all. Not with Big Ben at my side. Whoever it was had some girth though or the costume had a stack of padding.

We crossed the path where the Ski-Doos were parked and into the trees on the other side. We were ten yards from it now. It was making grunting noises like a bear and it was at this point that a sense of unease began to creep upon me. Next to me Big Ben slowed his pace as he too stared intently at the advancing killer.

Then it stood up.

The lump of shambling white fur pushed off the floor with its front paws and came to its full height. I estimate it had to be somewhere near nine feet tall, but the most striking and memorable feature were the two rows of teeth and two giant upwards facing tusks when it opened its cavernous mouth and roared at us.

Whatever it was, it wasn't a man in a costume!

Big Ben uttered a few choice words which I echoed and then we were both running away.

Quite definitely as fast as we could.

'That's no man in a costume, Tempest!' he yelled at me.

'You think?' I had seen down its throat and seen the size of its feet. They were images that would stay with me forever. 'Get to the bikes!' I yelled, meaning everyone.

Behind me the beast roared again. The sound loud enough to penetrate down to my bones and I swear I damned near wet myself when I heard it begin to charge.

Ahead of me, Jagjit, Hilary, and Francois were beating a path to where three of the bikes were parked. When we pulled up, Jagjit, Big Ben and Hilary had parked a little further down the path than Francois and me. The creature was coming at us from an acute angle, so our machines were closer to it than to us. We were going to have to double up but Jagjit and Hilary had already realised that and were going to get to the bikes first. Behind them, Francois was huffing and puffing as he too struggled to get to the Ski-Doos and the hope of escape.

I could already see that he wasn't going to make it in time. Old age and a calorie rich diet combined with a lack of regular exercise had made him slow. His heavy frame was struggling through the snow, but while I needed to save him, I couldn't imagine how I was going to fend off the beast or distract it.

The first engine fired into life quickly followed by the second as Jagjit and Hilary reached the Ski-Doos. Then, before Big Ben or I could shout, Jagjit got the third machine started and began beckoning urgently for Francois to hurry up. I risked a glance over my shoulder to find the Yeti was all too close. So, I did something stupid: I changed direction.

I also started yelling to get the beast's attention. I wasn't going to escape if it meant someone else didn't, and this had to be my best chance. It was no more than six yards from me when I turned to face it and waved my arms in its face. The huge creature swung its giant head and evil eyes toward me, then altered course.

It was coming right for me.

Questioning my sanity, I turned around again to start fighting my way through the snow once more. I had to buy more time. There was a large conifer ahead, if I could just make it to that, I would have a shield of sorts to hide behind. Big though it was, I doubted the Yeti could rip a tree from the ground. The shouts of my friends reassured me that Francois and Big Ben had reached the Ski-Doos and were safe. That left just me to worry about, but I knew they would come back for me now and try to distract the creature on the fast-moving machines until one of them could pick me up.

It was still a scary tactic, but as it turned out I needn't have worried because my friends left me behind.

The noise of the engines powering away down the track to safety made me eyes widen until I realised that Big Ben hadn't gone with them. No doubt he had given them his angry face and sent them out of harm's way. I had reached the tree and would later claim that I could feel the Yeti's breath on my neck as I ducked behind it. Half a second later a loud thump followed by a shower of snow from the tree told me the Yeti had arrived on the other side.

In theory, I could keep the tree between us forever and would be safe all the while so long as it kept circling it trying to get to me. Staying in the wood at the top of the Alps wasn't in my plan though. I had observed that the ground we were on had a good slope to it. Trudging through it was hard work as our feet went down to our knees with each step but maybe I could use the gradient to my advantage.

Big Ben was coming back to me now but running into the trees as I had meant he couldn't get close enough for me to climb on. The Yeti lunged from the right, but there was too much tree for him to get around. I just needed him to commit in one direction so that I could get myself on the same side as the track. Big Ben could see my game of cat and mouse and

64

had seen me indicate silently that he should stay where he was and be ready.

Almost a minute went by with the giant beast roaring and grunting its disgruntlement. It wanted to eat the tiny human, but the tiny human wouldn't run away for it to catch. Then, it grew bored and tried a tactic I hadn't considered.

I couldn't tell how many feet of snow there were, but there were enough that none of the trees had trunks. The snow came up to the branches, absorbing the lower ones so they all looked like Christmas trees planted six feet lower than they should be. The Yeti decided it was big enough to just go through the branches.

If I hadn't been too terrified to swear, I probably would have said something colourful. In truth though, I almost made a mess in my shorts for the second, third or perhaps fourth time in the last few minutes. The onrushing danger triggered another reaction though as I employed the tactic I hoped would save me: I turned into a penguin.

Throwing myself away and down the slope, I landed on my belly with my hands by my side and I slid. I had been worried that the snow might just give as I hit it which would have been the same as handing the Yeti a knife and fork, but my forward momentum carried me across the surface of the snow like a penguin sliding on its front. I wasn't heading toward the track and Big Ben though. I was just heading down the mountain and I wasn't sure how to steer.

There was a final roar from behind me, but I didn't look back. I was picking up speed and confident I had escaped. To my left through the trees, the sound of Big Ben's engine dopplered on and off as the sound tried to find its way to my ears. All I had to do was pick my way through the trees and across to the track. That proved harder than expected

65

though as the slope's gradient increased and my speed went with it. My attempts to right myself were thwarted by my forward momentum. Instead, I tried using my shoulder to steer like one would on a skeleton bob. It worked – sort of. But I was going to have to do something to slow myself soon or I would escape the Yeti only to crush my skull against a rock or tree I couldn't steer around.

All of a sudden, I burst from the trees into wide open space; I was back on the piste. Any jubilance I felt was quickly replaced though with the crushing realisation that the mountain really angled downhill sharply from this point. Big Ben's Ski-Doo emerged from between the trees behind me as the track also joined the piste and I risked a glance to see how far behind he was. However, the action of looking back over my left shoulder caused the right one to dig into the snow. I caught too much snow, my shoulder dug in with a jarring thud and I flipped. Like a professional downhill skier you see on TV when they are right on the edge of their ability and get it wrong, I became a tumbling windmill of arms and legs. If I had been a race car, this would be when I burst into flames.

Painful impacts registered all over my body as I tumbled and tried to keep my limbs tucked in. I couldn't tell which way was up, but I was slowing and soon enough I came to a stop. Out of breath, elated but painfully bruised nevertheless, I sat on the snow while my good friend Big Ben raced down the slope toward me. Like the good friend he was, and because I had just endured a crazy experience, he hit the brakes and swung his machine in a wide arc so it would stop it parallel to me and shower me with a wave of snow.

'Quit laying around, Tempest. We're losing the race back to the hotel.' I could always rely on Big Ben to be an arse. Sympathy for injuries wasn't something we would ever do for each other though, its just not the army way. Like, "You got shot? What do you want me to do about it? Try to avoid doing it again and get on with your job."

He offered me his hand to get up and pulled me onto the Ski-Doo behind him.

I offered a painful, 'Thanks, buddy,' as I grabbed hold of the machine and he set off back down the hill. The hotel was visible in the distance and I could see the other two Ski-Doos waiting for us maybe three hundred yards down the slope. They were not the dominant feature I could see though. The sky to our front had a cloud bank from which lightning was arcing. The blue sky above us was about to be eaten by the storm we had been warned about earlier. As I thought that to myself, the wind began to pick up and the first few fresh flakes of snow whipped by.

Big Ben powered the machine down the slope toward our friends and the police chief. They were waiting for us at a confluence of ski runs, off to one side and out of the way as skiers raced down the hill. As we neared them, Francois indicated to the sky in an urgent manner and then down the slope as he took off in his Ski-Doo with Hilary and Jagjit on his tail.

It was time to get inside.

We had made it back to the hotel as the winds were really picking up and the sun had appeared to set prematurely, the thick black clouds blocking it out almost entirely. All around the buildings of the resort, shutters were being closed over windows as they prepared for a battering. Snow was coming in thick, stinging lumps that felt more like hailstones, but none of us hung around to examine them. We rode the Ski-Doos into the underground parking garage we had collected them from just as men working there were closing the roller-shutter door.

Looking about and out into the storm, one of the men asked, 'Where are the other two?'

I guessed that he meant the Ski-Doos when I answered. 'Had to leave them behind. We'll go back for them when the storm passes.'

He flapped his lips a few times, trying to form an answer and looked ready to send us back out to get them when Francois took his hand and shook it, leaning in to whisper something quietly in the man's ear. The man's face registered shock as his eyes bugged out: Francois had told him about the Yeti.

I didn't want word to spread because I knew it would cause panic. There had been sightings of something that could be dismissed until this point. With the attack and death just a couple of days ago and now the police chief claiming to have seen it himself, widespread panic was likely. Had there not been a storm, the news would likely cause the resort to empty, but then I expected the cable car couldn't operate in these conditions and would be grounded so no one could get out until it passed.

Oh!

68

If no one could get out then no one could get in, which meant Amanda wouldn't get in. I checked my watch. She would have landed by now and be on a train probably. I needed to call her, but there was no signal in the underground carpark.

Now that we were all off the Ski Doos, we were all sort of looking at each other, each waiting for someone else to speak. It was Francois that broke the silence. 'Still willing to challenge the Yeti legend?' he asked. The question was directed at me and I was having a hard time finding an answer.

My immediate reaction was to reject the concept, but then what had just chased and threatened to kill me? Whatever it was, it wasn't a man in a costume. But a Yeti? The idea was ridiculous.

'It sure looked like a Yeti to me,' said Hilary. A sentiment that was echoed by Jagjit.

Francois added, 'I think we should be thankful there was only one of them.' I was still reeling slightly from the challenge to my base beliefs when he said, 'I shall have to shut the slopes to cut off its food source and organise a hunting party to catch and kill how ever many of them are out there.'

Its food source.

I smiled. 'How many animals live this far up the mountain? Are there any deer or elk or whatever is indigenous here?'

My question was clearly aimed at Francois, but Jagjit picked up on what I was suggesting. 'Yeah. An animal that size would need a sustained supply of food and I don't think it is a herbivore.'

Francois shrugged. 'There are rabbits and birds and a few other small animals. Nothing big though. Not this high up. It's permafrost, or for nine months of the year it is.'

'Shall we get inside, chaps?' I asked. We had been outside a long time and the ride down the mountain at a terror-induced velocity had added wind chill. I was cold enough to want to get into somewhere warm, so my friends were probably colder as both Jagjit and especially Hilary were slight and carried little or no body fat. I talked as we moved toward the door through to the hotel. 'I can't explain what we just saw. I will say that I don't believe it lives here and I refuse to believe that it is the same creature that attacked people here a century ago. So, it is something else. If there is no food source, then someone is feeding it.'

'How could anyone feed that without losing a limb?' Big Ben asked.

We pushed open the door that led from the corridor that connected the parking garage with the hotel reception and basked in the blast of warm air that assailed our faces. The reception and lobby of the hotel was half-filled with people, most of whom were staring out the large window at the front of the hotel to see the storm outside. There wasn't much to see as darkness has descended, but we could hear the wind whipping around outside and as we looked, a bolt of lightning, unseen in the storm, illuminated everything for a nanosecond.

'I need to find Anthea,' announced Hilary, throwing the rest of us a wave as he headed for the elevators. The ladies had taken themselves and a credit card to the hotel's spa this afternoon but were sure to be back in their rooms now.

Jagjit began to hurry after Hilary, saying, 'Yeah, I had better find Alice,' as he went.

Then Francois began crossing the lobby but was going backwards so he could look at Big Ben and me as he spoke, 'Whether that was a Yeti or not, I still need to close the slopes until it can be caught.' Then the crowd swallowed him, leaving just the top of him visible as he moved toward the doors.

I looked at Big Ben expectantly. Everyone else had already gone. 'I need to find some women,' he said, then looked over the top of my head at the skiers milling about. The storm had forced them off the mountain earlier than most of them would have planned and there were still people coming in now, though I could see the numbers left outside diminishing. 'There's some. Catch you later. Have fun with Amanda.' He stuck his thumb in his mouth and mimed blowing up his chest to make himself look bigger, then swaggered over to where a gaggle of twenty-something-year-old ladies were chatting.

'I doubt Amanda will get here,' I called after him.

He paused and turned, considering my statement, then worked it out. 'They'll close the cable car, wont they?'

I nodded.

'So, we're trapped here.' His eyes had a faraway look to them. 'I can use that,' he said as he turned back to the ladies. As I contemplated what my next move might be, I could hear him asking the ladies which of them wanted to be protected from the evil storm.

My next move was to go back to my room and check on the dogs. I couldn't take them outside in the storm so the parking garage would have to be their toilet. I would get some gear from the room to clean up/pick up any mess they left. I also needed a shower from all the frantic running through the snow and abject terror.

Upstairs, as I fumbled for my key card, the door barked at me until I got it open and the ferocious beasts it contained were able to establish that it was just me. They snuffled excitedly about my feet and jumped at my legs to be fussed. Ushering them inside, I closed the world outside so I could sit on the floor and give them what they craved. Normally, when I get home, they get excited and fuss about me but then want to be let into the garden so they can chase pigeons and squirrels and water the lawn. Since that was not an option, I clipped on their leads and collars and took them down to the garage. I wasn't too worried that their exercise level would drop. They were such lazy creatures that they rarely asked to be taken out and often hid when they heard me get their collars. A few days of hanging out indoors wouldn't bother them at all.

The parking garage was filled with cars though there was a gap where two Ski-Doos ought to be parked. I wondered how they would weather the storm, but believed they were heavy enough to resist the high winds. They could be dug out, restarted, and ridden back down when the storm had dissipated.

What about the Yeti though? I had been tussling with what I had seen since our escape from it. A nine-foot-tall, bear-like white furred beast with horns and tusks. The term I had for it was aberration. How could it be that a creature like that could exist anywhere on the planet without it being common knowledge?

It couldn't.

Surely.

So, what had I seen? It was troubling but I refused to believe that there was a Yeti and that it lived undetected in the mountains of Europe, venturing out to kill people when it got a bit peckish. Whatever the case, the police chief was right, and it needed to be caught. I suspected that meant they would shoot it and that didn't sit comfortably with me.

My musings led me around the car park twice as the dogs sniffed about and lifted their legs on the wheels of several cars. As I was leaving, a woman came through the door into the carpark being led by two more Dachshunds. The boys instantly perked up, pulling on the leads to meet the new dogs. Dachshunds are so rare in England that I can go months without seeing another but then I remembered Hubert telling me his wife had a pair.

'Madame Caron?' I asked tentatively. I hadn't met nor seen a picture of the woman so this could be her dog walker for all I knew.

'Oui,' she answered.

'Bonjour. I'm Tempest Michaels, the detective your husband hired,' I explained switching to English. I could have given most of the sentence in French but couldn't remember what the French word for hired was and had I done so, she might well have launched into a long sentence in French that I would have failed to understand.

As my dogs met her dogs and the four of them attempted to make a knot from their leads in their desperation to sniff one another, she leaned forward and shook my hand. 'Bonjour, Monsieur Michaels, Francois told me you all saw the Yeti that killed my daughter.' Mrs Caron looked terribly sad, filled with a grief she was barely containing. No tears came though, which I was thankful for as I never know what the right thing to do is in such circumstances.

'We saw something,' I conceded.

At my comment she tilted her head in confusion. 'You don't think it was a Yeti?' she asked.

I looked down at that point because the hand holding the dog leads was being yanked continually as the dogs played. They weren't playing though; they were having a four-way.

'Oh, goodness!' exclaimed Madame Caron because her little girls were being humped by my boys.

My immediate reaction was to break them up but then I considered that the little chaps got even less action than me and I was certain I wouldn't want to be disturbed at this point. Also, the girls appeared to be quite willing participants.

'Do we, ah… do we leave them?' I asked.

'No! Get them off, get them off!' Madame Caron demanded while tugging at her own pair of leads.

I said, 'Sorry, chaps,' as I reached down to lift each of them off the girls. Bull growled at me in a convincing way, or at least, as convincing as a dog the size of my shoe could manage. He was not happy. I looked back up at Madame Caron's horrified face. She was petting her dogs, one tucked under each arm and smooshed into her face as she cooed to them in French.

I replayed our brief conversation in my head to work out what we had been talking about when we noticed the dogs. 'Madame Caron, you asked me about the Yeti. My answer is that I don't know what to think. It is clearly not a man in a costume, but I am unwilling to assume that it is a dread beast that has so far defied discovery.'

'What about the pictures from the previous attacks. I have seen them myself. This region has a history of Yeti problems and there are probably more attacks than those we know about. People go missing here sometimes.' The last sentence was delivered in a hushed voice like it was a secret she wasn't supposed to talk about.

Bull and Dozer made a new attempt to get away from me by lunging in tandem. They wanted to get to the girls, but Madame Caron was unlikely to put them back on the floor until I had gone, and I felt that it was time for me to leave her alone.

I said, 'I cannot comment on old photographs and rumours. I will, however, investigate this case to the fullest of my ability and intend to reveal the truth.'

Madame Caron looked a little stunned at my statement. 'The only truth you will find is that my daughter was killed by a Yeti, Mr Michaels. I don't want you dredging up her past in your foolish quest for another explanation.'

A tear escaped her right eye and began to track its way down her face. 'Very good, Madame Caron,' I replied. 'I feel that this is not the time, but for my investigation I have some questions only you can answer.'

'You wish to interview me? Am I a suspect?' Her tone was defensive.

'Not at all, Mrs Caron. I just need to establish some facts.'

She turned to go, dismissing me as she moved away. Over her shoulder she said, 'Speak with the hotel manager, he will arrange a meeting.'

I called, 'Good evening.' As she left, then tugged the leads and led the dogs back into the corridor that would lead into the hotel reception. There were two things that stood out from our short conversation:

1. She used the distinct phase *"Dredging up her past."*

2. Michel Masson had not passed on my message.

As I pushed my way through the door and into the hotel lobby, I pulled my phone from my pocket and pushed the button for Jane. My office assistant was able to find information that most people couldn't. With something like this, I wouldn't even know where to start.

'Hey, boss,' she answered the phone in her usual deep voice. 'It's James.'

I had to mentally adjust what I was going to say then as my cross-dressing computer wizard had elected to dress as a boy today. He didn't do that very often anymore, preferring to wear girl clothes because he said they were more comfortable and his boyfriend preferred it. I thought it was all a little odd, but it was none of my business so I kept my mouth shut.

'James, I need you to do some research.'

'Of course. What have you got?'

'Well... what I thought was going to be a simple case of a crazy murderer dressing up turns out to be something else. Can you look up everything you can find on Yeti sightings, investigations, hunts and evidence of it existing in the French Alps, please?'

There was a moment of silence, then James said, 'Sorry, I was waiting for you to say you were only joking.'

'I wish I was. Something chased us today and it wasn't a man. Just pull together whatever you can that looks interesting and let me have it. That's a secondary task though. What I need you to do first is look into the two rival families here. The Carons and the Chevaliers. Focus especially on Marie Caron and anything embarrassing in her past.'

'Okay, boss. Anything else?'

'Yeah. How's it going?'

'At the office?'

'In general. I abandoned you to run the place again and now Amanda is on her way here...'

'Erm, about that. Is there something going on between you two? Not that you have to tell me, of course. I get that its none of my business, but you have both been acting differently around each other for a week now.' James lapsed into silence.

How did I answer him? I thought Amanda and I had acted as we always would, but clearly, we had been fooling ourselves. 'I, ah. We,' I started speaking but couldn't work out how to frame an answer that was both truthful but didn't tell him anything because we hadn't worked out what there was to tell yet.

James cut in, 'It's early days, right? Say no more. I won't mention it again. I'll get on with that research.'

'Thank you, James.'

'Boss?'

'Yes?'

'Good luck. I hope you two work out.'

Then he was gone. I thumbed the contact entry for Amanda.

'Hi, Tempest,' she said as she answered the phone. 'I'm almost at Tignes now but the weather outside looks awful.'

'Yeah, that's why I am calling. They have shut the cable car, so you won't be able to get up the mountain.' Amanda said a rude word in response. 'I don't know how long it will be shut for, but you will need to get on the internet and find yourself a place in Tignes to crash for the night. There's no chance it will reopen before the morning.'

'Dammit. I was looking forward to having a couple of days together.'

'Me too,' I agreed. 'But maybe it will only be one night, and you can get here tomorrow. I doubt I will be able to wrap this case up in the next day though, so I will still be embroiled in the Yeti case when you get here.'

'That's fine, I can join in. You have Big Ben with you already, don't you?'

'Yes, and Jagjit and Hilary.'

'Hilary? What's he doing there?'

'He's become Mr Spontaneous ever since the witch nearly killed him so he's here with Anthea having a few days off work for skiing.' I then filled her in on the day's events but deliberately left out the bit where I had almost messed myself running away from a giant Yeti creature.

'Sounds like an interesting case,' she said.

'Well, like normal, I have no idea what is going on yet.' Amanda and I spoke for several minutes back and forth. I think we both wanted to spend time in the other's company and this was the best we could manage. Neither wanted to end the call and it was almost as if I was a teenager again filled with out of control hormones. In the end, Amanda said she was arriving in Tignes and needed to go.

I wished her a good evening with a tinge of disappointment that I would not see her until tomorrow. 'What shall we do now?' I asked the dogs, but all I got back was grumpy faces which made me wonder how long it would be before they forgave me for breaking up their orgy with the girls. I took to a knee to get down to their level and pat their heads. 'I'll tell you what, chaps. If I can, I'll set up a date for you while we are here. How does that sound?' Bull cocked his head to one side, curious about what I was saying, while Dozer just wagged his tail. 'How about some dinner then?' Speaking a word, they recognised very well caused two pairs of ears to lift with interest. I took them upstairs and stroked their fur while they ate, then dealt with my own needs.

Evening was fast approaching and since Amanda wasn't going to get here, I figured I might as well head to a bar with Big Ben and the marrieds. I needed a shower and some food before that.

Three hours later, I was tucked in a corner of the bar waiting for everyone else to arrive. I was near the bottom of my second gin and tonic and feeling thoroughly relaxed about life. The dogs were tucked under my chair snoozing and twitching their legs and lips in little doggy dreams.

I had already eaten, having messaged Jagjit, Hilary and Big Ben in a group chat to ask them about dinner plans. I got back almost the same response from each them to the effect that they were having sex. The content of the message was sub-textual from Jagjit and Hilary but Big Ben, who wouldn't understand the concept of subtext, announced that he had scored with a lady and her mum and her aunt, adding that if I didn't hear from him before eight o'clock, I should send pizza.

I didn't bother to reply to any of them. Instead, and fighting a need to be moody because everyone but me was getting some, I ordered a large T-bone steak and asked them to send it out still mooing. The plate it arrived on was discarded on the other side of my table with nothing but a well-picked bone and a few spots of juice to show what had once been on it.

'Monsieur Michaels,' purred Michel Masson as he approached my table. 'I find you here looking all lonely when there is no need for you to be.'

My lip twitched with a tinge of annoyance, but I replied politely, 'Good evening, Michel. Can I help you?'

'I rather think it is I that can help you,' he replied as he reached into his jacket to produce a key card. 'In case you find yourself lonely in the night.' He placed the key on my table, winked and walked away.

His advances were beginning to bore me. I had said no and that should be sufficient. I moved to flick the card onto the floor, then thought better of it. Big Ben suspected his involvement in the case, though I wasn't entirely sure there was a case now but having a key to the man's room might prove useful later. I slipped it into a pocket, only then seeing that Michel was watching from across the room. He smiled and blew me a small kiss. Involuntarily, I rolled my eyes.

The storm was still raging outside, the wind quite audible above the music in the bar as it swirled and span, the buildings creating eddies as they blocked its path. I hadn't seen the police chief since we arrived back here several hours ago but left alone as I was, I had found time to compile a list of thoughts.

1. If the creature is not a Yeti, what is it?
2. How is it that the creature is seen so rarely when it is so big and clearly carnivorous?
3. Why is my client not more upset about the daughter he has yet to bury?
4. What is it the client's wife doesn't want me to find out?

And things to do:

1. Interview the wife properly in the morning
2. Get the fur sample analysed (where?)
3. Quiz police chief on his intentions in hunting the beast
4. Have James research Priscille Peran just for completeness and because I am curious about her story – why were they so far from the track that would have taken them to the slope they wanted?
5. Come up with a plan to catch the creature and hold it.

It wasn't a very long list, but I was still wondering whether I even had a case to solve. The creature we had seen either was or was not a legendary undiscovered Yeti, but it was certainly capable of killing a person. Had it torn poor Marie apart? If so, why had it spared Priscille? If the creature was responsible for Marie's death, then my investigation really had nothing to unravel. There would be no clever conspiracy behind the young woman's death, and I wouldn't feel I had any right to charge for my services beyond the expenses I had incurred for travel. Lost in thought, I didn't see the danger approaching until it slammed both hands on the table in front of me to make my heart stop.

'Alright, virgin?' asked Big Ben, a contented and smug grin on his face.

'I hate you. Please boil your testicles in vinegar and never bother me again,' I replied once my heart restarted. The dogs had emerged from under my chair to see Big Ben because they knew he would fuss them.

He looked up from patting their heads. 'Pint?'

I nodded.

'Good. I need something to eat and drink. I have worked up quite the appetite.'

'I don't want any details, thank you, Ben,' said Alice as she joined us, Jagjit holding her hand and also looking thoroughly satisfied with his evening.

'The Clintons are right behind us,' he said. 'Anthea went to complain about the towels in their room. Apparently, the cotton count is lower than she expects from this level of hotel.'

I wanted to comment but refrained. It sounded exactly like something Anthea would do, she seemed hard to please, but I didn't wish to voice my thoughts.

'I'll get a round then, shall I?' said Big Ben as he took a drinks order and headed to the bar

Jagjit pulled out a chair for his new wife. 'What have you been up to?' asked Jagjit.

I shrugged. 'I walked the dogs, I got some food, I thought about the case.'

'Yes,' said Alice. 'Jaggipoos told me about the Yeti. It sounded horrific. How are you going to catch it?'

An involuntary smile crept onto my face as my Indian friend's face coloured. 'Jaggipoos?'

'Yes, he's my little Jaggipoos,' Alice laughed.

'Oh boy,' said Jagjit. 'That's not going away any time soon.'

I had a broad grin now. Big Ben picked that moment to return with drinks. 'What's that huge grin about?' he asked.

I looked at Jagjit. 'Would you like to tell him, or should I?'

'Tell me what?'

It was Alice that answered, 'Tempest thinks my nickname for Jagjit is funny.'

'What nickname?' asked Hilary as both he and Anthea also joined us.

'Jagjit?' I prompted.

With a sigh of resignation, Jagjit stared at the ceiling and said, 'Alice calls me Jaggipoos.'

Everyone laughed, including Alice.

Big Ben said, 'Don't worry. None of us will call you that.'

I agreed, 'Of course not.'

'No, we'll call you poo face instead,' finished Big Ben to another round of laughter. As it settled down, Big Ben got Alice's attention. 'So, Mrs Jagjit, now that you are married is the sex suddenly boring?'

'Ben,' warned Jagjit.

'You're right, sorry,' he said giving Jagjit an earnest face. 'It was probably already quite boring before the honeymoon.'

'Ben,' Jagjit was doing his best to not be aggravated since that was Big Ben's intention. Alice was smiling though.

'When you need some tips for adding some spice,' Big Ben said with a wink. 'I'm a fan of the piledriver position myself. Have you...'

Jagjit reached for his pint with the clear intention of dumping it on his friend's head.

Big Ben laughed and ducked out of the way. 'Okay, okay,' he said as he hid behind me. Just making sure everyone is focused on Jagjit's tiny penis and not worrying about the giant scary snow beast. That's all.'

Inevitably this prompted a discussion about the case and the creature we had seen a few hours ago.

'What will you do?' asked Jagjit.

I took a sip of my drink as I considered my answer. 'In the morning, I will speak with Chief Delacroix. If he is arranging a hunting party, which I think he probably must, I will join it. I want them to use non-lethals to catch it. He will need to close the slopes until it is caught, I'm surprised he didn't do that already, but no doubt he was lobbied by the local businesses to take a minimalist approach after Marie's death. He lives here so it cannot be easy to make a decision that is going to hurt the pockets of everyone around you. Apart from that, I don't really know what to do.' I had a few sneaking suspicions about the people involved but none that were worth airing.

Just then the food they had ordered arrived. I had already eaten and my bladder was demanding I attend to my basic bodily needs. 'I'll just excuse myself for a moment, I think,' I announced getting up. I left my friends talking as I headed across the bar to rid myself of the excess liquid I had imbibed. The dogs stayed at the table, but with the food smells coming from the table, I would have been hard pressed to convince them to leave anyway.

The toilets in the hotel were just as refined and elegant as everything else. Standing at one of the urinals, staring at the wall as one does, I sensed movement behind me. A toilet flushed and then another one almost immediately afterward and I heard two of the toilet doors open. I paid no heed to the men behind me as they moved to the basins and washed their hands. But when one spoke, he got my attention immediately.

'I say, Stefan, does that gentleman not look familiar to you?' the voice asked.

'I dare say he does, Arthur. In fact, I would go as far as to say the gentleman looks exactly like that tosser, Tempest Michaels.'

Thankfully, my task was complete, so I zipped up and turned around to face the voices. I knew the two men, but I couldn't say I was pleased to see them. I had first met them a couple of months ago when their boss was hunting a vampire.

My upper lip curled in a sneer as I addressed them, 'Arthur, Stefan, I didn't know the circus was in town. Where's Vermont?'

It was Stefan that replied, 'That's a good question,' he swished his long, almost floor-length coat back in a move that was intended to make him look like he was getting ready for a fight. 'A more interesting question would be: where is your big friend?'

I grinned at him then. They felt confident because it was two against one. 'Don't you remember attacking me in my office? Do you have a good memory of that event?' I didn't feel a need to remind him that I put them both on the floor in about six seconds.

Stefan grinned back though. 'Yes, I remember. That's why getting even will be so much fun. And this time we have these.' With a flourish both men produced knuckle dusters and spread their feet to better distribute their weight for fighting.

I felt my pulse quicken. It was an involuntary reaction which always made me angry. I didn't want to fight these two idiots, but I wasn't being offered an option. Stefan took a pace to the right, his fists up as he began to circle. Wisely they were trying to split my attention. I wasn't going to wait for them to decide they were ready though. I was going to hit one of them so hard his head exploded.

Just then the door opened. All three of us had our fists up and were a heartbeat away from throwing punches, but the two men coming through the door were chatting and hadn't looked up.

The two men were Jagjit and Hilary.

Arthur noticed that my attention was split and lunged for me, a haymaker punch swinging in with a glint of brass on the end of it. From the corner of my eye, I saw Jagjit and Hilary's expressions change. I had no time to yell for them to get out though, I was too busy ducking back to avoid the knuckle duster opening my cheekbone. Unfortunately, ducking one of Vermont's henchmen forced me towards the other.

Stefan though was good enough to aim his punch at my kidney, the blow stunning me as he put everything he had into it. As I reeled from that, I caught a foot to my midriff that threatened to double me over. I had to get control here or I would be in trouble, but it turned out I was worrying unnecessarily.

As I lashed out a sweeping arm to create space into which I could move and looked for a limb to grasp, Hilary slammed into Arthur and Stefan vanished under a blanket of Jagjit. The guys had come to my rescue, both of them taking on bigger men that were likely to do them harm. Suddenly I was the only man standing, everyone else was on the floor, two pairs of men struggling for a dominant hold. It wouldn't take long for Vermont's henchmen to gain the upper hand though and I couldn't allow that.

A voice roared from the doorway, 'Enough.'

Yet again, I knew who it was without having to look.

'Stefan, Arthur, what is the meaning of this?' demanded Vermont Wensdale. Both men stopped moving or at least stopped fighting and did what they could to stop Jagjit and Hilary from doing them any harm as they stopped resisting.

I turned to look at Vermont, but he wasn't alone. Faces were appearing behind him, drawn by his shout. Big Ben was visible above all the other heads outside, but Alice and Anthea saw their husbands on the floor and shoved their way into the gents.

I gave the guys a hand off the floor but left Stefan and Arthur to get themselves up.

'Are you alright, baby?' asked Anthea of Hilary as Alice cooed over Jagjit. Both ladies had joined their husbands to check they were okay.

'I'm fine, angel,' Hilary replied. 'Tempest was being attacked.'

She shot me a sneer as she said, 'You're so brave,' and kissed him.

'What are you doing here, Vermont?' I asked.

'There is a beast to catch, is there not?' He was wearing his usual uniform of tight leather trousers and a sleeveless silk shirt with a cape. His feet were in fancy, thigh-high boots that he might have stolen from a Musketeer.

The crowd peering through the toilet door parted as Big Ben pushed his way in. 'Am I going to have to give you another beating?' he asked as he came into Vermont's personal space and looked down at him. Vermont is a big man, tall and muscular, Big Ben is just, well, taller and more muscular. There was so much tension in the room I was half expecting to see static electricity arc between the two men.

Vermont took a dramatic step back though and from somewhere behind his back he produced a sword. 'This sword was given to me by a Benedictine monk. One of the nails used to pin Jesus Christ to the cross is worked into the hilt and the blade itself was quenched in holy water as it was worked. This I will use to slay the beast which threatens the lives of the people here.'

'How about if I cram it up your butt?' offered Big Ben.

88

I heard a scream then. Everyone else heard it too. From the hotel lobby maybe, the sound hard to pinpoint from inside the toilets, but the crowd outside were no longer looking in and they were beginning to disappear from view.

A shout from outside sounded like someone had said, 'It's the Yeti.' We had been frozen in time for a second, but the shout galvanized everyone into action, the small door becoming a logjam as we all tried to fit through as one. Exploding through the doorway and into free air, Vermont bellowed for room, ramming his way through the crowd to get to the lobby area.

There were more screams ahead and as we were trying to get to the front of the hotel and the double height windows there, the people at the front were trying to get away from it. Vermont pushed through them, using his sword to scare people into moving out of his way and I followed on his heels, slipping through the gap he made.

The storm was still raging outside. It was as black as it could be, but the lightning was still flashing intermittently to illuminate the snow falling and swirling. As Vermont and I barged through the last line of people, a bolt of lighting provided a freeze frame of outside and there was the Yeti. On its back feet, standing to its impressive full height once more and snarling to the sky. Then it was gone, swallowed by the darkness once more.

The sight had caused my jaw to drop in awe, but Vermont didn't even pause. His charge forward continued. 'Stefan, Arthur, it's slaying time,' he called through gritted teeth as he touched something to his neck which released the cape. The cape fell to the floor in his wake as his henchmen also pushed through the crowd.

The madman was actually going outside! He didn't even have a coat on.

'Vermont, you fool! You'll freeze!' I shouted after him.

At the door he turned to face me, a smile on his face. 'God will keep me warm, Mr Michaels.' Then calmly, he pushed open the door and vanished into the storm.

I turned to look at the crowd of people watching the spectacle behind me. Stefan was just coming through the last of them but hadn't noticed Big Ben who stuck out a helpful foot to send the man sprawling across the tile.

'Don't go out there,' I implored both Stefan and Arthur as they tried to follow their boss.

'Step aside, weakling,' spat Arthur.

So, I did. Both men visibly steeled themselves against the cold, then they too vanished into the night.

Big Ben walked across the lobby. 'They were fun. Shame they're all dead now. Shall we eat? I'm starved.'

I stared at him then stared out the window again. How long could they survive outside? I didn't know the answer, but I was willing to bet it was measured in minutes. I shrugged. Big Ben was right, everyone else had food getting cold at the table and there wasn't a thing I could do to help Vermont.

I clapped Big Ben on the shoulder. 'Let's eat then.' With a shared smile, we both took a step toward the bar area. The crowd was beginning to disperse, confused and scared faces wondering just what was going on, but the din of conversation carried one word continually: Yeti. We had gone two paces before the door behind us flew open again. A fresh savage blast of frigid air cut through the lobby as I span around to berate

Vermont for endangering himself and his men, but it wasn't Vermont trying to push the door shut. It was the police chief Francois Delacroix.

Big Ben and I rushed to help him close the door as others ran down to join us, including Michel Masson.

'Francois,' he said, 'what is it?'

The police chief's face was grave as he turned to us, 'We've been trying to account for everyone that was on the slope today. It's an almost impossible task because there are so many directions you can ski and stop.' I didn't like where this was going.

With dread understanding, Michel asked, 'Who is it?'

An echo rippled around the lobby as the conversation was overheard. Everyone realised there were people that hadn't made it down the mountain.

Francois's shoulders slumped. 'I have checked with all the other resorts. I think Remy Bernard and Andre Thomas are still on the mountain somewhere.'

'Then we have to form a search party right now,' Michel was already turning to address the crowd when Francois snagged his arm.

'We can't, Michel. It's too dangerous and the mountain is too vast. We have to wait for the storm to pass and look for them in the morning.'

'They'll die if they're exposed,' he countered.

'And everyone else that goes out there will die from exposure trying to find them,' Francois calmly replied. 'We have to pray they found shelter somewhere. They are villagers so they know how to survive in the cold.'

The conversation was being followed by the guests in the lobby, but no one was arguing with the idea of staying inside. Resigned, Michel nodded his reluctant agreement. 'We must make arrangements to set out at first light. The storm will have blown through by then.'

'You are probably right, Michel,' agreed Francois. 'Have everyone meet at my office, we will assign search areas and check people are dressed correctly before anyone sets off. I don't want more casualties from well-meaning hotel guests. I'll spread the word. Ask for volunteers, but,' Francois held up a warning finger, 'I want fit and able-bodied people. I don't want children and pensioners.'

Big Ben shot me a glance to check before saying, 'Count us in. We've both had Arctic survival training and have lived through worse than this.'

Francois accepted his offer gratefully. 'I have to go. There is much to do. First light,' he reminded us as he pushed the door open again and went back out into the night.

Michel faced us. 'How's the investigation going, boys? Francois told me you saw the Yeti up close today.'

'We did,' I admitted.

Then he said, 'I have work to do, please excuse me.' He began to move away, then stopped and signalled to a female member of staff that was working in the restaurant. She scurried across, throwing a quick smile at us and then turning her attention to her boss. Michel said to us, 'This is Lissette. She is the bar manager.' Then he turned his gaze to her. 'Please attend to these gentlemen's needs.'

Big Ben whimpered with excitement, the noise escaping his lips to reach the lady's ears. As Michel hurried away, Big Ben fixed her with a meaning-laden smile. 'I believe that in all the excitement, our food has gone cold. Would you be a dear and arrange for replacement meals, kitten?'

Her mouth opened slightly as she stared up at him, her tongue slipping out to wet her lips, 'Oui, Ben.'

'Call me BIG Ben,' he commanded.

She sucked in a quick gasp of air as she wilted beneath his smouldering gaze.

I just walked away.

Back at the table Jagjit and Alice and Hilary and Anthea were looking at their cold plates of food with disappointment. 'Order fresh,' I advised them. 'The bar manager will take care of the bill.'

'Are you sure?' Anthea asked.

I inclined my head. 'Pretty sure, yeah. Though it won't be until after she climbs off Big Ben.'

'Urgh,' she made a small sound of disgust. 'Is he at it again? All that man does is chase women.'

'I don't think many of them try to run away,' replied Jagjit with a frown.

'Really?' said Alice having seen her husband's face. 'I'm not enough for you?'

'Hold on,' Jagjit was taking umbrage. 'A few minutes ago, I was a hero for tackling a henchman twice my size and your poor baby because I have a fat lip. Now I'm in trouble because I have a friend with magic power over ladies' underwear?'

It was time for me to exit before the marital bliss got flipped on its head. 'I'm going to bed. Where are my dogs, please?' I actually knew where they were. They were still tied to the table and straining to get to me. I bid my friends goodnight, took the dogs for another walk around the underground carpark, which I can tell you was significantly colder than the rest of the hotel, and went up to my room. Just as I got there, the older man in the room next to me was just getting back. He was stripping off outdoor clothing and had clearly been outside from the snow stuck to his gear.

'Have you been out in the storm?' I asked.

He met me with a smile and said, 'I, ah. I don't...' I waved him to silence and apologised for not being able to speak his language.

'Deutsche?' I asked but got a head shake in return. 'Russkiy?'

'Da!' he replied, pleased for some reason.

I didn't know what good evening was in Russian, so I patted his arm and went into my room. I had a box of gravy bones with me which I had placed on a table that I believed the boys couldn't get to. They hadn't done so far but give Bull enough time and he might work it out. They ran to sit beneath the table now, staring at it then staring at me and then staring back at the place they knew the treats were again. I fished out two biscuits for each dog, let them crunch them and get a drink of water, then plopped them both on the bed and dealt with my own needs.

It had been a long day and I had slept in a car last night so I was not only tired but feeling less supple than I usually would. I turned the taps on to run a hot bath and scratched my head while I yawned. There was still no service on my phone so I couldn't even text Amanda.

I reminded myself that she would arrive tomorrow. We would be together soon enough. In the meantime, I needed to reconsider my plans. I wanted to interview Mrs Caron in the morning, but the search would make that impossible. I could look for her when I returned though.

The Search. Thursday, December 1st 0530hrs

The hotel lobby was decorated for Christmas when I came down in the morning. Overnight, Santa's little elves had been very busy erecting a tree that must have been eighteen feet tall and they had suspended streamers that spoked out from the top of the tree to every point in the room. Tinsel adorned every surface and there were decorations hanging in abundance from the walls.

It didn't feel like Christmas. As a single man I paid little attention to the season and had missed countless Christmases in the army because on December 25th I was hiding under a rock somewhere watching for an enemy that had no idea what Christmas was any more than I could name their religious holidays. But I knew my sister put her decorations up overnight so the children came down to the magic of it on December 1st and guessed that if I had kids I would get caught up in the excitement too.

I had awoken early, and it had been dark in my room, but the dogs had woken me because they needed to go out. Crossing the lobby on my way to the car park, I could see that snow had piled against the glass front and doors of the hotel. It was five feet high and would take several men with shovels to clear it, but the storm had gone, and all was calm outside again. I didn't know what time first light was, but now I was up I wouldn't go back to bed even though the dogs would be done in just a few minutes. There were a pair of young men trapped on the mountain somewhere and I was going to do my bit in the bid to find them alive. With luck, they had found somewhere to hide from the storm and this morning would awaken to the most amazing fresh powder runs, arriving jubilant and unharmed back in the resort before the search parties even set off.

I hoped that I wasn't being too hopeful.

The dogs, always keen to get somewhere, were dragging me across the lobby to the door that led to the carpark. There was no one else around at this time of the day to see me in the ski jacket, crumpled joggers and running shoes I had thrown on in my haste to get the dogs out before one of them peed on the floor. I didn't even have socks on, which I regretted the moment I opened the door to the carpark and the cold hit me.

It had to be five below zero in there. The dogs didn't pause though, they were on a mission with a pressing task to perform. Checking around, I unclipped their leads and let them run off to explore. I hadn't been checking to see if there was anyone to see the dogs peeing on car tyres, I had been making sure there was no one around to see me shiver like a weak civilian. The cold air bit at the exposed skin around my ankles and penetrated the single layer of my coat in about three seconds. Hugging myself to stay warm and encouraging the dogs to hurry up, I thought some more about the case and wished I had battery heated underpants.

Dozing off to sleep last night with the dogs curled against my hip, I had rerun all that I knew and tried to look at it from different perspectives. A woman had been killed. If it was deliberate, then who stood to gain? Asking the question though just felt foolish because I had met a nine-foot-tall monster that would have killed me too if I hadn't escaped. Surely, that was what had happened to Marie Caron. Was I just wrong about there being a criminal behind her death? I had slept dreamlessly, waking with the question still on my mind. There was a monster here, I knew that much. All the evidence pointed toward her death being nothing more than misadventure, but I wasn't here to track and kill a Yeti.

In many ways I should have expected to be wrong at some point. My career success was founded on the principle that there had to be a rational and non-paranormal explanation for every mystery I faced. That didn't appear to be the case this time.

But what had they been doing so far from the track? I kept circling back to that question.

The dogs trotted back to me, the cold driving them to be quick about their business. I used baggies to deal with the necessary, depositing it in a bin as I left the frigid car park behind. Coming back through reception, I met with Hubert. He was dressed in head to toe ski-wear and carrying gloves and a hat with fold down ear muffs.

'Good morning, Mr Michaels,' he said with a small wave of greeting.

I returned his greeting, then asked, 'Will you be joining the search party?'

He nodded gravely, his expression telling me what he thought about the young men's odds of surviving the night. 'I knew them both. I might not have liked them, but the villagers here are a community, and we pull together when we need each other. Their families will want all the help they can get.'

'When is first light?' I asked.

'In about an hour. It's earlier here because the light is amplified by the snow and it will hit the side of the mountain above us to light that long before it begins to cast shadows here. There will be a hearty breakfast laid on for all those joining the search. I have a team setting that up in tents by Francois's office now.' That meant I had plenty of time to get ready and to prize Big Ben out from under his collection of ladies. I thanked Hubert and took the dogs back to my room.

Hubert hadn't asked me about the investigation. Perhaps he was preoccupied with other things. Usually though, my clients are all over me for updates, wanting to know what I have found out, what I can reveal so far. He didn't seem interested at all.

An hour later, I left the room and knocked on Big Ben's door. The dogs were tucked up again with full bellies and empty bladders and were going to sleep through the morning without the slightest concern for my whereabouts. I had checked my phone but there was still no signal. Whatever damage the storm had done might take hours to fix or maybe it would take days. It seemed quite possible Amanda would find me at the resort before I got to speak to her.

From deep in his room, I heard Big Ben's voice calling in response though I couldn't make out what he said. I shouted that I would meet him in the hotel lobby and went there to wait. I didn't want to see who he had in his room this time. Thankfully the hotel was built to last and had thick walls so any noise he had been making last night hadn't penetrated through to me.

Downstairs, there were a few dozen people now moving around and drinking hot fresh coffee from the restaurant where staff were up and handing out warm croissants and pain au chocolat. It was still dark outside but when I crossed to see what people by the doors were looking at, I discovered they could see the sun hitting the very tip of the mountain above us. It was astonishingly beautiful. From this angle, we could only see the one mountain peak out of the hundreds the area contained. Outside, where the full spectacle of the Alps could be seen, the view must be spectacular. No one was going out though because the staff were still trying to dig their way to the doors. We could see over the top of the snow to a team of men working hard with shovels near the hotel entrance while noise from snow-blowing machines was shifting it in volume further afield.

I grabbed some hot coffee, the caffeine welcome at this time of the day and then drifted back to the doors as the men outside were nearly done. They would be warm despite the cold, their exertions probably making them sweat beneath the layers of clothing they had put on.

'Hey, Tempest,' said Jagjit from behind me. I turned my head to find him dressed in much the same gear as me. 'Alice is just getting coffee. Where's Big Ben? Or is that a silly question?'

'It's a silly question, but I expect he will be along soon. There's breakfast waiting for us at the rally point. Is Hilary coming?'

'No. I think Anthea talked him into staying here rather than joining in the fun again. They came around with leaflets last night inviting people to join in if they were able, but Anthea said there would be plenty of volunteers and he should spend some time with her. I got the impression it wasn't worth him trying to argue. You had gone to bed by the time all this happened though.'

I had. Fatigue had driven me to take an early night and I felt refreshed from it. There was a knock on the door and the muffled shout of the man outside as he called for someone inside to open the door. The man nearest the door looked confused until a member of staff pushed through the crowd with a set of keys. Outside, the black had become very dark grey as the sun fought back the night and soon we had joined a crowd of about one hundred people assembled by tents from which hot breakfast was being handed out.

Francois was moving among the crowd asking if people were carrying weapons. I watched as he held out his hand for a pair of men to hand over kitchen knives, then he raised his head to address the crowd in a loud voice, 'This is a search party ladies and gentlemen. We are not hunting the Yeti. I will send for a team of appropriately trained and armed marksmen from the city to hunt the creature once the cable car is operational again. I must ask that you do not bring weapons with you today.'

'Why not?' called a voice from the crowd.

'Does anyone have a rifle or high calibre long range weapon?' the police chief asked. Then he slowly turned on the spot, scanning the crowd for any raised hands. Seeing none he said, 'That's why. If you are close enough to use a knife on the Yeti, you are already dead. Today we will be searching in large groups, each group led by one of our mountain safety team. In the unlikely event that the Yeti is seen, the search party will get back on its snow cat and move away. No one will be in any danger as long as there are no fools carrying weapons.' Then he lapsed into silence and drifted back to a table and raised map of the area he was using as a gathering point.

Another question from the crowd stopped him. 'Why aren't we searching from the air?'

He didn't have to answer though as several new voices explained that we were far too high and the air all too thin for helicopters to fly.

'Did I miss much?' asked Big Ben when he found us, a coffee in one hand and a croissant in the other. 'Sorry, been up half the night, I'm starving now.' As he continued to shovel food in his mouth, Francois began addressing the assembled volunteers with a loud speaker. We were to be divided up into groups that would each search different areas of the mountain. They had twenty-seven Ski-Doos and six Snow Cats, large, tracked vehicles that could carry half a dozen people. These would be used to get to one of the search areas to deploy the searchers inside.

Radios were handed out and the groups were divided up. Francois continually reminded everyone to stay safe and be wary of the fresh powder. He had to deliver the briefing in three languages which probably still didn't cover the diversity of the crowd but took up enough time anyway. By the time we set off, the sun was lighting the mountain and we were no longer standing in the dark. It would be a while before the temperature improved though.

I noted that there was no sign of Vermont, but just as I had that thought, I heard his voice. 'Anyone spotting the beast is to report it to me,' he shouted in both English and French. 'I have a five thousand Euro reward for the person that leads me to it.'

'Where's your magic sword, Vermont?' I asked. He looked at me then as if noticing me for the first time, but he didn't answer me, instead he produced the sword from a sheath on his back with a flourish. Obviously, his hunt for the Yeti last night had proved fruitless but at least today he was dressed more appropriately in full winter gear like everyone else. Arthur and Stefan flanked him as always, their particular outfits stylised to match their *just escaped from the Matrix/vampire hunter* fashion with long leather jackets where the rest of us wore ski-gear. They were an odd pair but then with Vermont for a boss, their outfits were in keeping.

Big Ben, Jagjit and I had been assigned to a group that would drive some of the Ski-Doos. Francois said he knew we could drive them so the three of us set off first, getting paired with Gils and Gerard Chevalier, the rival hotel owner and his son whom I had already met, and one of their ski instructors whose name I didn't catch. She was petite and probably had a pretty face though it was hidden beneath a hat and goggles and a snood thing that covered her mouth so only the tip of her nose was showing. She got Big Ben's attention nevertheless and I saw Gils observe their exchange with a concerned frown as if Big Ben were touching his property. Curt pleasantries were exchanged as Gils politely asked if we knew how to operate the machines, they were his after all he pointed out unnecessarily.

'Still here?' he had said when we approached the Ski-Doo he was sat astride. 'I thought you would have gone home after your run in with the Yeti yesterday.'

I tilted my head to the side as I met his eyes. 'How do you know about that?' I asked.

He opened his mouth to answer but paused as if he didn't know the answer, then replied, sounding almost flustered, 'It's a small village. Everyone knows everything.'

I pursed my lips but decided not to pursue it. 'Well, I saw a creature I couldn't identify but I have not been convinced the creature killed Marie Caron. Until I do, I remain here.'

'What,' he scoffed, turning to his father on the Ski-Doo next to him. 'He thinks there's a murderer in the mountains and the Yeti is just a friendly woodland creature.'

His father pulled down the scarf that covered his mouth, then smiled broadly as he said, 'I dare say he does, Gils. Let's hope we don't see him today anyway.'

I didn't rise to their goading, there were more important tasks to focus our effort on, but I saw Big Ben squinting at Gils as if trying to decide whether to say something or not. I guess he filed the insults away for later as he took another bite of his croissant and chewed it slowly while continuing to stare at the back of Gils's head.

Francois finished organising the crowd into groups and set the search party in motion. Gils waved his hand as he twisted his throttle. Then he pulled away, his father following and the rest of us peeled off to form a snaking line as we set off up the mountain.

The call to tell us the search was over came at 1047hrs. They probably would have been found sooner but the deep snow that fell overnight hampered everything the search party were attempting to do. It was Hubert's team that had found the bodies, the news that they were dead quickly followed by a report that they had been killed not by the storm but by the Yeti. Big Ben and I exchanged grim looks and the ski instructor made horrified noises until Big Ben calmed her with a strong arm around her shoulders that might have been what she was angling for anyway.

Each group only had one radio, ours was controlled by Gils, so I asked him, 'Where were they found?'

'At the bottom of Trevalle Bluff. It's on the western face on one of the black routes. Why?'

'Because that's where we are going. I need to see the site for myself.'

Gils cranked his throttle to swing his machine around and position it in front of mine like the top of a tee. 'No. You'll be coming back to the hotel now. These Ski-Doos are expensive to maintain and run. The search is over, which means play time is over.' He swung his head around and stood up in his seat to address everyone. 'We're heading back down now.' Then he looked right at me, using his extra height so he could look down. 'That means you too.'

I laughed. I hadn't really meant to but watching him try to intimidate me was funny. I raised my voice, 'Ben.'

'Yup?' he had been comforting the ski instructor still, his head down and probably whispering something in her ear until I called.

'We are off to see the attack site. Are you ready?'

'No, you're not,' snapped Gils.

104

I leaned forward on my handlebars to get in his face. 'I'm not sure what is motivating you, Gils, but unless you plan to wrestle this machine away from me, I am going to the attack site. They may need a hand there, but either way, I am here to conduct an investigation and that is what I am going to do. Trying to stop me will not profit you in any way.' I was going to add that the Ski-Doo would be returned shortly and in the same condition it was in now and that I was happy to pay for the fuel or even a rental charge, but I didn't get to that bit because he tried to hit me.

Maybe he just wasn't used to being argued with or challenged or maybe he is just a bully, but his arm shot out toward my jaw and I was well within striking distance.

Big Ben caught it easily though, hooking a hand into the crook of Gils's arm as he threw it forward. Gils had been focused on me, and with a padded helmet on, he hadn't heard my friend walking up behind him. Gils's face registered surprise before Big Ben levered upward to yank the man from his Ski-Doo and dump him on his arse next to it.

'Wow,' said Alice who was riding as a passenger of Jagjit's machine.

The motor of Gils's machine was still running so Big Ben climbed on, abandoning his own where he had left it, twisted the throttle, and pulled away saying, 'Shall we?' As he headed back the way we had come. I quickly caught up and took the lead since I had a rough idea where we were going. One advantage of a long army career is you learn to map read from topography. Like everything else, if you practice it, you get good, so I had more or less memorised the map of the mountains and had been able to navigate using the two largest peaks to get my bearings.

As we chewed a path through the snow, I wondered if Gils might race after us to continue the fight, but when I looked back, they were nowhere in sight.

Navigating to the site was surprisingly easy, not because I had a compass inside my head, but because we could see it when we reached the top of the very first rise. They were two-hundred feet below us and half a mile away with the sun on our backs. It still took over an hour to get to it, by which time Francois had been joined by Hubert and another team of searchers that had been designated an area not too far away. The hotel guests that were among the volunteers were waiting to be taken down the mountain but there had been staff from the hotels, and villagers that worked in other businesses that had been pressed into digging the bodies out.

It was grim work and tiring. Big Ben saw what was going on, the two of us joining the work party soundlessly except for a word to keep Jagjit and Alice with the Ski-Doos. It wasn't that I thought them too weak to handle it, I just didn't want either of them to see sights that would stay with them forever. Big Ben and I were already scarred.

Most of the work was already done though, the bodies were no more than a few inches down in the snow where they had fallen. It was at the edge of a short drop so the air was blowing over it, making the snow thinner there. It was pink in places, no doubt that was how it had been spotted. Francois was standing near the feet of one of the bodies, not moving, not speaking, just staring at it silently, the cold breeze coming up the hill making his wispy hair flutter. The sun had warmed the mountain and was amplified by the snow reflecting it. It was cold only when the wind blew.

As I joined him, he turned to see who it was. I got a rueful nod of his head as he said, 'I have to tell their parents. I see bodies every year. There is always a climber that falls or someone that ignores the warning signs and skis where they shouldn't. Or there will be a paraglider that hasn't

107

checked his equipment. It's never been someone I knew until this week though.'

The young man on the icy ground in front of me was barely recognisable as human. Only his clothes gave it away. His face looked like it had gone through a woodchipper. I forced myself to focus on the details as I picked a clean bit of snow to kneel in. Leaning over the body, I could inspect the wounds. 'Can I touch him?' I asked without turning my head.

'Yes,' Francois replied. 'Just don't move him. I need to take photographs yet. Hubert sent for my camera equipment. The storm knocked out the phone lines and damaged the cable car so the coroner cannot get here until we fix it. I have to catalogue the scene and arrange for the bodies to be removed and stored until I can transfer them.'

I was thinking about the logistics of it when I realised what he had said. 'The cable car is broken?'

'A tree came down and hit the cable. They have to perform a one hundred percent inspection of the cable millimetre by millimetre before they can allow it to run again. It will take at least a day and far longer than that if they find any damage.'

I bit my lip in frustration. I wasn't going to see Amanda any time soon, but I had two dead men in front of me that would laugh at my petty concerns. I tuned myself back into what I was doing. The wounds I could see did not look machine made, nor did they look like knife wounds or bullet wounds or any type of wounds I had ever seen. If I had to give an answer, I would have said they looked like bite marks. It was a gruesome sight. I wasn't sure what I was looking for, but when I saw it, I had to force myself to not react. It was the clue I was mostly praying I would not find, but there it was and since it meant I could no longer trust anyone here, I kept it to myself.

I moved to the other victim looking for the same piece of evidence and I found it instantly. Now that I knew what I was facing, and my worst fears were confirmed, I needed to speak with my assistant Jane more than ever. She would be able to delve where I couldn't and probably find out who was lying to me and who was not.

How long would the phone line be down?

I wanted to stand up to ask the question out loud because I believed that if there is a God up there, he has a massive sense of irony. I didn't bother though because even if he did pick that exact moment to fix the phones, there would be no signal at this altitude anyway. Instead, I left the poor young men behind me and returned to my Ski-Doo. On the way there, I spotted something in the snow. Where the loose powder was being blown around, there was a line in the snow leading to the bodies. I knelt to inspect it. The line was a deep depression in the snow that was mostly hidden by the fresh powder but had been cut into the older snow beneath. It was four inches across and went on as far as I could see in both directions. I couldn't actually see all that far because the powder was covering it and wouldn't have seen it at all if I hadn't stepped over it. The unnatural appearance of a straight line had drawn my eye though. Now that I knew it was there, I followed it a little way, losing it under the fresh snow then spotting it again where the snow was thinner. It led away from the attack site and down the slope in the direction of the resort.

So, what was it?

Curious, I tried to find another one running parallel. I judged the distance and began wafting the powdery snow away with my hands. I had to be gentle so I wouldn't destroy the mark while I was looking for it but I found nothing. Undeterred, I tried on the other side of the track, striking gold almost immediately and now I had a pair of parallel tracks that left a deep impression in already compacted snow.

'What have you found?' asked Francois. I hadn't heard him approach but for once the surprise didn't make me jump. I hadn't wanted him to see but now that he had, I really didn't want him to realise that he was suddenly among my long list of suspects. I showed him the two tracks. 'What do you think made it?' he asked.

'I have no idea. I am not given to believe in coincidence though.'

We exchanged a glance but were distracted by the appearance of three more Ski-Doos coming up the slope on a direct path for us. They were riding in an arrow formation and I could already see that it was Vermont Wensdale with Arthur and Stefan flanking him because of the capes and long coats flapping behind them.

'Heads up,' I murmured to Big Ben as I got back to my machine. The sound of the approaching party hadn't reached anyone else as the breeze was carrying it away, so I was the only one on the slope that had seen Vermont coming. Big Ben swung around in his seat then yawned to show his disinterest in a kind of, "fought them before, beat them, can't be bothered to teach them another lesson," kind of way.

'Do we stay?' Big Ben asked.

'Only long enough to check they are not going to cause Francois any trouble.' After saying that, I watched the police chief cross to the Snow-Cat tracked vehicle and wave it off. It was taking the hotel guests back but was leaving a small party of others behind. I could see those still here were staff from the hotels as they each had on one of two different coats, each with the emblem from their hotel. It was worth noting that despite the two owners hating each other, the staff bore no animosity or rivalry at all. Or, if they did, it had been set aside to deal with the more pressing matter of finding and now caring for the two young men.

'Check for tracks,' Vermont instructed his henchmen as he skidded to a stop. He paid no attention to anyone else as if all others were so insignificant that he didn't see them. However, as Stefan and Arthur fanned out, their eyes on the ground, Vermont made a beeline for Francois. 'The beast has claimed two more victims, yes?' Francois nodded but didn't reply. 'Then time is of the essence. This beast will not stop until it is slain. It is a good thing I came.'

He turned to see what his men were doing. 'Anything?' he called at a volume they would hear. Arthur held up a hand. I had no idea what he might have found but he was way over to the left of us and appeared to have found something because Vermont raced over to him on foot, then the pair of them came back for their machine and within two minutes of arriving, they had gone again.

'He sure is entertaining,' observed Jagjit.

I couldn't argue with his statement, but said, 'Let's get back. I have research to do.'

My quest to speak with Mrs Caron didn't get very far, or more accurately, it failed to get me a result. Michel Masson, the hotel manager assured me she was not in the hotel but assured me he had passed on my previous message and would do so again. There wasn't much more I could do in pursuing her, so I put the task off again and sought out some food.

As I finished my sandwich, a rumour the phones were back up spread through the restaurant like wildfire. All around me, people pulled their phones out and started to check them. The air was filled with beeps as messages, emails and other notifications landed all at once. I was among those with my phone in my hands, eagerly checking to see if I could now connect with Amanda.

My French onion soup and bread was left to cool while I read the messages that had just landed. I had several texts from Amanda starting at 0803hrs with a breezy, "Good morning." Shortly after that she must have learned that the cable car was out because that was what her message was telling me. I elected not to read any more of them and called her instead.

'Tempest,' she said suddenly as if she had snapped up the phone in desperation to speak with me. 'Is everything alright?'

'The cell tower got knocked out. The phones have been down until now. Otherwise, the answer to your question depends upon one's perspective: there have been two more deaths.'

I heard her take a sharp intake of breath. 'Two more? And are they supposed to be Yeti attacks?'

'Yeah, about that. My theory that it would be a man in a suit?'

112

'Yeah.'

'Well... it's not.'

I could almost hear her cogs grinding as she processed that bit of information. 'It's not. So, what is it then?'

'A YETI!' I delivered with a ridiculous vaudevillian cackle. I switched my voice back to normal to say, 'Whatever it is, it is not a creature that exists as far as the planet is aware and it chased and almost ate me yesterday.'

'Definitely not a man in a really good costume?' she questioned. I would have questioned it too if I hadn't seen it.

'It was somewhere near nine-feet-tall and opened its mouth when it roared at me. It is not a man. This thing had a mouth whose bite might have to be measured by radius. A bit like my mother,' I added.

'Wow. Okay. So, what are you doing now?'

'I'm still investigating. Regardless that the creature blamed for the deaths is actually a creature, I am not buying the idea that this is some undiscovered monster that has lived in the Alps undetected for centuries.'

'What is it then?'

'I haven't worked that bit out yet,' I admitted. 'But I looked at the latest victims and... look I can't talk openly because, other than my friends, I don't know who I can trust. I need to speak with Jane and get her to do some more research. I have a few specific questions to ask her.'

'Understood. Have you any idea how long it will take them to fix the cable car? The station at this end is closed and no one else seems to know anything.'

'They told me it would be many hours because they have to inspect the whole length of the cable. I guess they don't want people plunging to their deaths. If they find any damage it will be days before it reopens, I guess.'

Amanda swore quietly. 'Let's take it a day at a time then. I'll stay here until tomorrow, but if the indication then is that it is not about to open, I will accept defeat and go home.'

I sighed. 'This is annoying.'

'Yes, it is,' she agreed. We talked for a bit and then she let me go because I had work to do: Jane had emailed.

Boss,

There wasn't much to find on the Chevaliers or the Carons other than family history and mundane facts about their business interests. No one in either family has a criminal record, everyone was educated to a high level and Gils Chevalier graduated from the Sorbonne summa cum laude for law and business. There is nothing about a feud between the two families that I could find.

The Yeti has several reported incidents across the Alps

1832 B. H Hodgson's Yeti Report

1889 Major Waddell's Yeti Prints

1903-1904 British Army Shoots a Yeti

1913 The French Snowman

1921 September 22nd Colonel Hogarth-Boynes's Yeti Sighting

1922 William Knight's Yeti Sighting

1923 Major Cameron's Experience

Please see attached document for full list

I began scanning the entries but did not read them all as there were so many. Opening one at random, I read that Colonel Hogarth-Boynes had seen and given chase with his Lieutenant when they rounded a rock formation and spotted a tall creature with white fur. His report was detailed, even noting the time at which the event occurred. The Yeti legend was already established so he was most likely seeking notoriety for killing the beast and presenting it to the world as his trophy. Given that the time was listed as early evening, I suspected it more likely he had been at the gin in the Officers' Mess and had imagined the whole thing.

Jane's report then switched to Marie Caron; the person I had asked her to pay special attention to.

Marie Caron attended the prestigious Institut Villa Dellareui in Paris which was where she met Priscille Peran. I have attached a photograph from their graduating school year but couldn't find one that listed names beneath each girl. I was able to lift the social media profile for her though so I have provided the best head shot I could find. A chunk of her past is missing. About eighteen months ago, all her social media feed across all platforms is just gone but until then she was prolific. It slowly started coming back after a gap of nearly four months. I figured this was the smoking gun I was looking for and I will admit it took some

115

convoluted digging to find it through other contacts in her friends list.

It would seem that Mademoiselle Caron engaged in a spot of Ménage a trois with two young men who then published pictures all over the internet. I have attached what I found but there is so little out there that someone must have gone on a hunt to eradicate the evidence. The two men are Remy Bernard and Andre Thomas and their home town is listed as Harvarti.

I stopped reading at that point. The two dead boys had been murdered, that much I was certain of. I just had no idea how the killer was pulling it off. Remy and Andre had posted pictures of a naked Marie they were both entwined with. I flicked briefly through the pictures Jane had sent me, finding one of them both high fiving over Marie's back at which point I worked out what the term Eiffel Towering meant. Their decision to post the photographs had brought embarrassment to the Caron family and someone had sought their revenge. Was my client the one behind it all? How could that be true? He was the one that had employed me, so if he were covering up a crime and using me to deflect attention away from him, then was my death a part of his plan?

The thought sent a chill through me, I had brought Big Ben here with me, Jagjit and Alice were on their honeymoon and Hilary was here with Anthea. Were they all in danger? They were all sitting around the same table as me, an empty bottle of red wine discarded to one side and a half empty one that wouldn't last long was in the middle of the table. They had just eaten lunch, and all looked happy and content even though the presence of the Yeti meant there might be no more skiing for the rest of their stay. They were chatting about it in positive terms because the Yeti story would be something for them to talk about back home – *you'll never believe what happened on our honeymoon.*

'Ben,' I called softly across the table to get his attention, then motioned with my head for him to follow me. He was texting on his phone, probably to the ski instructor from earlier, but put it in a pocket as he rose to follow me.

An area of chairs in the lobby just across from the reception desk provided a fresh place to sit where we would not be overheard. Only one old lady was sitting there, the book in her hands had a French title which reassured me that I could talk in her presence without needing to worry.

Big Ben sat in a chair opposite mine. 'What's up, buddy?'

'There's more going on here than we realised.'

'When isn't there?' He had me there.

I tried to order my thoughts before I continued. I was catching glimpses of different elements of the whole of this case but had yet to find a focal point that might tie them all together. 'We need to get a better look at the boys' bodies when they bring them down the mountain. Francois can't get them to the morgue with the cable car inactive so they will put them into a cold store. Tonight, we need to find where that is and break in to do an autopsy of our own.'

'Sure,' he nodded, willing to accept what I was telling him and follow my lead. 'Can you tell me why?'

'Both of the victims had marks around their wrists where they had been tied,' I saw Big Ben realise what that meant. 'I want to get photographs of the wounds and see if they have any other injuries. I also want to find a microscope somewhere so I can examine the fur we found.'

'What's going on?' asked Jagjit. I hadn't seen him approaching but he wasn't alone.

'Yeah,' said Hilary. 'You guys are being awfully secretive. I thought us men were in this together.'

'Hah!' laughed Anthea. 'When you have quite finished with the macho rubbish, you had better count us in as well. Isn't that right, Alice?'

'Welllll,' said Alice.

'Damn right,' Anthea said before Alice could give her opinion on the matter.

I looked around. Usually it was just me on these cases or sometimes me and Big Ben. Now I had a squad and I thought back to my earlier concern about them being in danger here. 'Gather round folks, I'll tell you what I know.' We all came into a huddle as I explained my thoughts.

'You don't know much, do you.' Anthea pointed out helpfully when I finished. I think she had planned to say that no matter what I revealed, but in this case, considering we might be targets, she was right.

'So, let me see if I have this right,' Jagjit started. 'You think that the Yeti isn't a Yeti but is something else, but you don't know what yet and the three people it has killed have all been murdered by someone who is using the legend of the Yeti to cover up the murders. Is that about it?'

Alice said, 'You missed out the bit about the Yeti being under someone's control and the possibility that the man that hired you being the killer.'

'Don't forget my favourite bit where the client and the police chief are involved in a conspiracy to murder his rivals, the Chevaliers or perhaps frame them for the murders,' added Hilary.

I waved them into silence. 'Okay, okay, you think this is farfetched? Amanda just solved a case where she had aliens tampering with the milk while it was still in the cows.' I faced a sea of bemused faces. 'What I am saying is; this sounds incredible to you, but for me it's just Thursday. I get this every day.'

Jagjit nodded his head in acceptance. 'You plan to get to the victims tonight and find some evidence?'

'That's the plan.'

'I can do that with you,' he volunteered.

'What about Marie Caron?' asked Hilary.

I pursed my lips and shook my head. 'Her body was taken away on the day it happened. Her mother identified her from a birth mark, but I don't think an autopsy was conducted. Whatever the case, we can't get to her.'

'What do we do between now and when we go sneaking about tonight?' Jagjit asked.

'We make a weapon.'

I felt like Hannibal Smith of the A team as I outlined my plan and sent the squad in different directions to perform tasks. We were all to meet back in the Honeymoon Suite in four hours or however soon we could get things done. After dinner, a select few of us would break in to see the bodies and get the evidence that they had been tied up and fed to the Yeti. Before that of course we had to find out where the bodies were going.

Jagjit and Alice were going to find me a microscope if there was one here to be found. I judged that there must be, there was a pharmacy after all. Big Ben was to set up an observation post to watch for Francois returning with the bodies so we would know where to find them tonight. Anthea would research ingredients required to make a tranquiliser and Hilary was going to work with me as we found parts to make the weapon.

As everyone headed in different directions, some were giddy with excitement at the mission they felt they were undertaking and others, like Hilary, were just feeling a bit sick. He said, 'I thought you were going to see if the police chief had access to a tranquiliser gun.'

'I was.' It was what I had suggested I would do when I brought the subject up last night. 'I'm not sure I can trust him.'

Hilary didn't like that. 'If you cannot trust the only policeman in the resort, who can we trust?'

'Each other,' I replied. 'He might be completely innocent, but someone tied those boys up and it was the police chief's group that conveniently found them. Their bindings were removed by the time I arrived, which could have happened as soon as they were dead. Or might have been just before we got there. I just don't know.'

'Okay then, how on earth do we make a weapon to shoot and knock out a Yeti in the space of a few hours?'

'That, my friend, is a good question. The answer to which is only part formed in my head.' That I didn't have a set of engineered plans to show him clearly worried him even more. 'Look, I find that having an exact plan works so rarely that I don't bother making them. I have a rough idea of what we need and how it should go together, I just haven't had to do anything like this for a while.'

'Since you were in the army?' he asked.

I just nodded as we walked. 'The first thing we need is a propellent, something that will fire the tranquiliser darts. This should do nicely.' Bull had stopped to sniff a pair of fire extinguishers. One was water and the other was CO_2. The water-based extinguisher was no use at all, but the carbon dioxide would provide a blast of gas. 'We'll need a few for testing so grab another two from different points in the hotel and bring them back to my room. We'll assemble the components there, okay?'

'Isn't that dangerous?' he asked. 'Taking the fire extinguishers, I mean.'

'Only if there's a fire.'

He conceded the point and left me to find two more while I grabbed a second myself and put them in the room. Over the space of the next hour, we found bits of pipe in different gauges, duct tape because you can fix anything with duct tape, springs, chunks of rubber and all manner of other paraphernalia we might need including a toolbox that I liberated from a corner of the garage where they kept and maintained the Ski-Doos.

Jagjit sent a text to tell me they had a microscope but the chemist in the pharmacy wasn't going to let them take it anywhere no matter what they offered him. I replied with an acknowledgement and advice that I would be with them shortly.

'How's Anthea getting on?' I asked over my shoulder as I tried taping a fire extinguisher to a piece of pipe. I was on the carpet with pieces of junk we had collected spread all around me. The dogs had seen me sit so had taken that as an invitation and climbed onto my lap. Now I was balancing two Dachshunds on my legs and trying not to snag their fur with the duct tape.

Hilary made an *I don't know* face but went to check while I continued playing with my makeshift gun. As he left the room, I hefted it and gave the extinguisher an experimental pull on the trigger. A blast of gas shot from the end of the pipe. I was going to need a shoulder strap though. Looking around, I wondered about using a belt then remembered the bath robe hanging on the back of the bathroom door. The belt on it was easy to tie and then tape in place so I hefted the pipe and fire extinguisher combo again. This time it was easier to use but I was shooting from the hip rather than the shoulder so aiming was going to be hit and miss. Unless I made it so it went over my shoulder and someone behind me aimed by looking down it.

That might work.

What I really needed was a projectile to try out. Behind me, the door opened again as Anthea came in trailed by her husband. She said, 'I have a list of ingredients we need that we might be able to find here. They are all complex pharmaceutical products that we will have to get from the pharmacy though.'

'Like what?' I asked.

'For starters we need an opioid. I had to read a whole bunch of advice to understand even what I was reading, but everything starts with an opioid. Then, how you mix it depends on the type of species you are going after.'

'How so?'

'Well, for carnivores it is common to use a cyclohexamine like ketamine combined with a sedative like midazolam or diazepam.' I had been listening while I continuing to fiddle with the gun but looked at her now to confirm she was reading from notes and hadn't memorized the complex names.

'What else,' I prompted.

'Actually, we can probably get away with Ketamine and diazepam if we can find them in a large enough quantity. We need to know what it weighs though in order to calculate the dose,' Anthea explained.

Hilary's eyes widened. 'Babe, this thing isn't going to get on a scale for us. Its weight is really heavy. Like half a ton or something.'

Anthea was right though. 'Overdosing it will kill it?' I asked.

'Don't give it enough and it will just get woozy and distressed and probably be more dangerous, too much and you stop its heart. Somewhere in there is a sweet spot where we can knock it out for a while. How long will you need?'

I sniggered at myself. 'I have no idea. I don't even know where to find it. Not yet at least, but I do have an idea about that. I'm heading to the pharmacy now with the fur sample I have. Shall we all go?' Two minutes later, with my room looking like a junkyard and the dogs leading the way, we went in search of Jagjit and Alice.

Outside it was almost warm. The breeze through the centre of the small resort village had dropped to nothing and the sun was blazing down from a cloudless sky. For the first time since we arrived, the dogs were happy to be outside. Their paws were sinking in the snow but the snowblower machines had been used to clear routes between the buildings so foot traffic could easily pass, and they were skipping happily along in their normal excited way. Bull stopped to sniff a piece of snow that he thought smelled of something, then lifted a back leg to sign his name on it. It wasn't attractive but he had to go somewhere and everywhere was white.

The pharmacy was easy to spot with its internationally recognised white cross on a green sign. It was a small place that doubled as a supermarket as shops do in tiny resorts. Jagjit opened the door as we got to it; he had been watching for us in anticipation.

'How's the weapons factory going?' he asked as the dogs dragged me inside, then he caught my expression. 'Don't worry, the owner doesn't speak a word of English. Alice has been translating.'

'Good,' I replied. I didn't think it a good idea to publicise my attempts to build a gun. 'We need drugs to make the tranquiliser and something to dispense it with but otherwise I think I have something that might work. It just needs some testing.'

'What drugs?' he asked.

'I have a list,' said Anthea as Hilary shut the door behind her. 'It's not a long one but I doubt the pharmacist will be willing to hand over the things I want.'

Jagjit looked confused. 'Why not?'

'Because they are barbiturates and opiates and can be used to kill people in the correct doses?'

He looked at me for a second, then grinned. 'Oh yeah. Come on, he's in the back.'

Alice was with him we discovered when Jagjit led us into a room just behind the counter and cash register. The counter doubled as the pharmacy dispensing area. It was all very bijou.

'Oh, hey, guys,' Alice looked up and greeted us as we went in. The pharmacist in my head was going to be an old man with grey hair and pair of bifocal glasses. In contrast to my expectations, he was twenty something, wide in the shoulder and narrow at the hip from time in the gym and had a mop of scraggly black hair that complemented his grungy skier look. Around his right wrist were thin leather straps he had tied, there were more around his neck and a silver earing in just his right ear.

I said, 'Bonjour,' as I went in. Then said, 'I have some fur to examine,' as I held up the small baggy it was in.

He laughed and rattled off something in French that I didn't understand, but he moved to the other side of the small room and pulled a cover from a microscope I hadn't even spotted.

'I told him we had something we needed to look at when he refused to let us take the microscope. He kept asking what it was, but I wouldn't tell him. He is asking again now.' Alice explained. 'What do you want me to say?'

'Tell him I found some fur near one of the attack sites and I want to know if it is fake or real.' Alice translated, which made the man's eyebrows reach for his hairline. He held out his hand for the little plastic bag I was holding but I didn't hand it over, it was precious evidence. Instead, I selected a single strand to carefully present.

He pursed his lips but said nothing as he held it up to the light then put it between two thin pieces of glass to slide under the microscope lens. Seconds later he was jabbering in French again.

Alice listened, asked a question and then looked up at our expectant faces. 'It's animal fur,' she explained, which to be fair, I already knew. Then she said, 'He thinks he can narrow down what genus it is.'

'Tell him all I want is a photograph of the cross section of the hair. Can he do that?' I asked.

While Alice translated, Jagjit whispered a question, 'Why don't you want to know what it is?'

'Because I think I already know, and I don't want anyone else to know that anyone else knows.' He frowned at my poor explanation, 'I will have to explain later.'

The pharmacist shrugged at Alice's request and began doing something complicated with the microscope.

I leaned to whisper in Hilary's ear, 'We will have to shoplift the drugs we need. I'm going to get him to show me something outside and you two will need to snag the drugs from the shelves in here while he is distracted. I will come back and pay him once we wrap this up but I can't ask for them without giving the game away.'

He didn't look happy about it, but he nodded his compliance and began whispering to Anthea. She shook her head emphatically. Thankfully, the handsome, trendy pharmacist pushed back his chair and began babbling in French again as, with a smile, he dodged by us and went out into the shop.

'He sent the picture to the printer in the shop next door,' said Alice following him. 'He also said it's on the house because I am so nice.'

'Oh, did he really?' enquired Jagjit. He stared at his wife with mock jealousy for a moment, before adding, 'You know I can speak French too, right?'

Alice giggled as she followed the pharmacist out of the back room, closely followed by her husband. 'We'll wait here then?' I called after the departing figures as Jagjit chaperoned his wife to make sure the other man didn't get any ideas. My French was rusty but even I knew the man hadn't used the French word for nice when he complimented Alice. He didn't look back as he left his premises though, I guess it was the laid-back hipster/skier persona that made him so relaxed but Anthea, Hilary and I all stared at each other for a split second, then burst into action and started raiding his shelves.

No one was watching for his return though. 'You two keep looking,' I called as I took up post in the front of the shop. Hillary and his wife were being as tidy as thorough and as fast as they could as they scanned the shelves and picked up boxes to inspect.

'I found Diazepam,' shouted Anthea. Then two seconds later, 'I have the Ketamine as well.'

'Get more than one. I don't know how much we will need, and we need some kind of spring-loaded syringe to deliver it.' I continued to watch for Alice and Jagjit returning with the pharmacist, my heartrate booming in my chest as the clock ticked away.

'There's nothing here,' Hilary called through.

I called back, 'There's still time. Keep looking, please.' A spring-loaded syringe. Basically, I wanted them to find a tranquiliser dart. Why would a pharmacist stock those? I had failed to think this all the way through. How was I going to get the drugs into the animal if I couldn't shoot them from a safe distance? Maybe it is a lady Yeti, I thought, in which case I can just get Big Ben to seduce it and we can jab it in the bum when it's not looking. Grinning at my own joke, my heart stopped as I heard the pharmacist's voice behind me.

They were coming through the back door!

The dogs spun around and barked loudly, doing their best to alert me to the presence of a person as they always did. Alice saw my panicked expression and was bright enough to understand what it meant. She had been following behind the man but snagged his arm now and looped hers through it in a flirtatious way. He stopped talking as, surprised, he looked down at her arm touching his and then glanced at Jagjit; the man clearly wearing a gold ring that matched hers.

Alice was using her arm, looped through the other man's as it was, to steer him around the shop. I couldn't translate what she was saying fast enough but she seemed to be asking him questions about his life and his skiing prowess. I heard him telling her that he preferred snowboarding, but I could still hear the Clintons opening drawers and cupboards in their search and clearly he could too as he kept swinging his head across to look in the direction of his back room.

I saw his facial expression change as he reached a decision and tried to pull away. He was going to catch Hilary and Anthea raiding his shop and that was going to be hard to explain.

Then two things happened. I guess Hilary heard voices because he poked his head out just as Alice got the pharmacist's attention. I watched his eyes flare before he ducked back into the small room out of sight. The second thing was that Alice distracted the pharmacist by grabbing his chin to pull it around to look at her and then stuck her tongue in his mouth as she proceeded to snog him.

The noise from the backroom stopped but I guess they didn't know what to do because they didn't come out and Jagjit did a very passable impression of a volcano about to erupt as his new wife kissed another man two-feet in front of him.

Alice broke off the kiss and let her arms fall to her sides. I hoped the tactic had given Hilary and Anthea enough time to put things straight because the moment the pharmacist's senses caught up to him, he dashed across the shop and into the back room from whence we then heard an explosion of inventive French swearwords and a tirade of abuse in return from Anthea.

I was stunned, rooted to the spot and unable to think up a reasonable lie to explain any of what was happening. I didn't need to though. The next second, Anthea came out of the back room, her clothes all askew and what looked like her knickers in her hand, dragging Hilary along behind her as with one hand he tried to pull his trousers back up.

They had been pretending to have sex! Or maybe they had actually been having sex. I couldn't tell but it was clear the pharmacist bought it as he yelled abuse from the doorway of his back room. Some of the abuse was aimed at Jagjit and Alice, who he labelled in turn as a sex-mad slut and a weirdo that liked to watch his wife with other men.

It very much felt like time to leave and I doubted we would be welcomed back if we realised we needed something else. I was nearest the door, so I held it open for Anthea and Hilary to waltz straight out of without breaking stride. They were followed closely by Alice who looked thoroughly embarrassed and by Jagjit whose expression was mostly set to murderous.

'She did the right thing,' I whispered as he went by.

The door swung shut behind me as we escaped across the snow with our drugs and our picture. I was at the back of the group which was moving slow and all looking at one another nervously. At my feet, the dogs were bouncing along quite happily and completely unaware of the tension sparking between the two couples.

Then Anthea burst out laughing. 'Oh, my God. I thought we were busted when we heard your voices in the shop.' She fixed me with an accusing look. 'I thought you were standing watch at the door to warn us.'

'We came in through the backdoor,' supplied Alice before I had to defend myself. Then she asked unabashed, 'Were you two really doing it?'

Anthea's cheeks coloured as she shook her head, but it was Hilary that spoke, 'I didn't know what else to do. I just thought: if he thinks we are back here having sex he'll be too horrified to question whether we were doing anything else.'

Everyone was laughing with relief except Jagjit. 'Are you okay, sweetie?' asked Alice. 'You know I needed to distract him. I couldn't think of anything else that would do it.'

'Mmm-Hmmm,' he replied. Alice had her arm looped through his now and as they walked, she leaned in to whisper something in his ear that made his eyes dilate and his rigid defensive posture wilt. Whatever she had just told him looked likely to mean we didn't see them for an hour when we got back to the hotel.

It transpired that both couples abandoned me to continue my investigation, each making a separate excuse for needing to return to their room. Momentarily, I was glad Amanda wasn't with me because then I too would be getting nothing done. I closed my room door behind me and settled in front of the laptop on my desk as the dogs scampered to their water bowl and then back to me to demand a treat.

With a sigh, I put the envelope with the photograph down again to fetch the dogs a gravy bone. Failing to do so would have escalated their insistence until, ten minutes from now, they started barking their disappointment at me. Instead, they contentedly crunched the biscuits to dust and slipped into the covers of my bed.

As my laptop came to life, I pulled the picture from its sleeve and set about the next stage of my research.

An hour had slipped by when I got the call from Jane. I had sent her the photograph in an email by taking a picture on my phone. I hoped the quality was enough to work with. Having sent the email, I called her to pass on several research tasks as I continued trying to work out a drug delivery method that didn't involve me holding the tranquiliser while the Yeti swallowed my arm.

Now she was calling me back. 'Jane, hi. What have you got for me?' I knew it was Jane because we had spoken today already. She would be sitting at her desk in the Blue Moon office on Rochester High Street wearing Ugg boots because it was cold and the stuffed bra she had taken to recently. I often found myself wondering why I didn't think it was weird that the man I hired was a girl more often than not.

'Hi, boss. Which bit do you want first, the good news or the bad news?' she asked.

I shot back instantly, 'I'm a dessert first kind of guy.' I wasn't of course, I didn't eat dessert, but it was just a thing to say.

'Well, there is no good news so...'

I sighed, 'Go on, tell me what it is.' Task number one had been to use the microscope picture of the hair to identify the creature it came from. I had been rolling the question around in my head for a day and had decided that I already knew what it was even though it no longer looked like it should. The height, sheer size and the size of its mouth were clues that when added to the white fur covering its body eliminated every creature on the planet except for a polar bear.

'It's a squirrel,' said Jane.

'Wait, what now?' I was certain I hadn't heard her right or that she was pulling my leg. It was nine feet tall, it had huge paws and I had googled polar bear prints to discover they looked just like the ones in the snow here.

'It's a squirrel,' she repeated. 'The Sciurus arctos carolinensis to be exact, which is a squirrel native to the Alpine region of Italy, France, and Switzerland. Most noted for its ability to change the colour of its coat when the snow thaws. That's not what you were expecting to hear, was it?'

I had found squirrel fur in the bark of the tree. Damn I felt stupid. All that subterfuge and it was a squirrel. It didn't matter. I still had a giant animal to capture without causing it harm and I was ninety-nine percent certain it was a polar bear. Well, ninety-five percent. Maybe ninety, but the point was that it wasn't a Yeti. The annoying voice at the back of my head was laughingly asking how it was that my polar bear had horns and tusks and had wandered about three thousand miles south.

'Boss, are you still there?' Jane asked, breaking my reverie.

'Yes. Yeah, sorry. No, I wasn't expecting to hear that the fur came from a squirrel. What about the other information I asked about?'

'I am nearly there with that, but I have a file I can send you now. The short answer is that both the Carons and the Chevaliers own a number of other buildings in and around Harvarti. The ski-lifts that run up and down the mountains carrying skiers to the top of the runs were almost exclusively owned by Hubert Caron until about five years ago. It would seem he had been offering the tickets to his guests for free but anyone staying at the Chevaliers hotel was charged a high premium to use the service. Monsieur Caron continued to raise the price until Gerard Chevalier took him to court and got an injunction. After that, Gerard had some of his own ski-lifts built so now both men own maintenance sheds and the like and there is at least one on each ski-lift run. There are also, I want to call them lifeguard towers, but I know that's not right, but whatever the safety guy equivalent is on a ski slope? Well, they each own some of them. I am sending you a list of buildings with grid references so you can find them.'

'Okay,' I said as I checked my emails. As I looked, it popped in. I opened it and saw the list. There were twenty-seven locations to check. Too many to tackle by myself when the ski-lifts were all closed. I would have to narrow it down some yet. 'Thanks for this as always, Jane. How's it going back there? All quiet?'

'Um, it's okay, I guess.' Jane's reply was tentative as if there was something to tell me that she had chosen not to tell me yet. I trusted her enough that I didn't press her to come clean. I promised to let her know how the case went and told her Amanda had found herself stuck in Tignes when she asked whether the two of us were getting any time off to spend with each other. When I heard a knock at the door, I bid her goodbye and disconnected the call. I had little choice because I couldn't hear her over the noise the dogs were making.

'Open up, loser,' called Big Ben removing any need to ask who it was. The dogs were still barking until I got the door open and showed them who it was.

'How'd you get on?' I asked as he came in, the two dogs following on his heels.

He thunked into an armchair with a satisfied grin. 'Just finished shagging Claudia.'

'Who's Claudia?'

134

He gave me a confused look. 'The superhot ski instructor chick from this morning? Have you forgotten her already?' Of course, he had already had sex with her. It had been hours since they were introduced after all.

'I thought you were watching for the police chief to return with the bodies so we would know where they are.' I pointed out while trying to keep the exasperation I felt from my voice.

'Yeah, I got lucky with that. He turned up with them on a sled covered in blankets about three minutes after I got outside to watch for his return. He has them stashed in the cold room of the Chevalier's Hotel. That's how I bumped into Claudia again. I followed them at a safe distance to see where they were going, then, when I saw them put the sled inside the cold store, I slipped away again but met Claudia as she was going into the hotel. You can probably guess the rest.'

'Let me guess. You smiled at her, and her knickers fell off.'

'More or less,' he conceded. 'So, how's the weapon manufacture going?'

'I have a machine that will fire a projectile using compressed gas. I tried it with a bar of soap I formed into a ball. That's how I got the dent in the wall over there.' His eyes tracked where I was pointing to a very obvious indentation in the plaster. 'I haven't worked out what I can use that will dispense the drug once I shoot the Yeti though.'

'Did you get the drugs already?'

'Yup. Anthea and Hilary found everything we need at the pharmacy across the road.'

'Well done them. Where are they all anyway?'

'Engaged in marital activities, I think. They all seemed to get quite a buzz out of the subterfuge required to obtain the drugs and get the fur sample analysed. Interesting result from the fur sample though.'

'Oh?'

While Big Ben listened, I explained about the ferocious squirrel we had to catch. He laughed so hard he almost wet himself. Then we settled down with a map and Jane's list of buildings to see if we could piece together some more of the puzzle.

As arranged, after dinner Jagjit and I set off to check on the bodies of the two young men. Big Ben had said there was no guard on the cold store when he was there, but he came with us just in case there was one now. Of course, when Big Ben said he was coming, so did Hilary because he didn't want to be the only man that stayed at home nice and safe. Then the two ladies had asked if the men thought it was too dangerous for girls and I backed away from that conversation fast I can tell you.

So now, my surreptitious night excursion was a full-on group outing. I should probably be glad the ladies hadn't brought drinks and nibbles. The new plan, which I hastily concocted on the go was for us to have a couple of drinks in the bar at the Imperial Hotel. Jagjit and I would then slip downstairs to the cold store located in the Imperial's underground car park under the pretence that we were looking for the gent's toilet should anyone discover us.

The plan went sideways about eight seconds after arriving in the bar.

Gils was there and he hadn't forgotten or forgiven Big Ben for dumping him on his butt earlier. He rose as we crossed the room to order drinks and find a table that would seat the six of us. The bar was busy, much busier than the bar in Hubert's hotel, the hubbub of conversation making the music being played barely audible. Then it lulled as half the women in the room spotted Big Ben as he walked in, their heads turning and their conversation faltering as they observed and assessed. He was used to it because it happened everywhere he went, so ahead of me, he paused and gave the room a top level, knicker-melting smoulder.

As I caught up to him, he whispered, 'Look at all these cherries to pick.' He meant women of course and he was right in that the ladies in the bar outnumbered the men by what must have been close to two to one.

137

'There's a cherry, and there's a cherry, ooh, there's a nice juicy one.' He was already heading in a different direction when he said, 'I'm off to pick it. Won't be long.'

I muttered a few choice words as I followed the marrieds to the bar. That was when I spotted Gils moving across the room on an intercept course for Big Ben. Instinct altered my course, not that I thought Big Ben would need my help dealing with Gils if he planned to start a fight. My intention was to ensure Big Ben only hit him once. In some instances, you are not given the option to avoid the fight, but only hitting a person once, if that is all it takes, is a very defensible position. The prosecution cannot argue that you were enraged or intending harm. One is a non-divisible number. You cannot hit a person less times than once.

I didn't have to worry about Gils though because someone else got to Big Ben first and there was nothing I could do about his first attacker. He had reached the table at which his juicy cherry was sitting. She was sitting at a table for four with two other lady friends. I was too far away to hear him, but as I closed the distance, I watched him smile and introduce himself and take the spare seat.

Then, a woman sitting at the table next to him rose to her feet, picked up her drink and threw it in his face. My feet, or perhaps common sense took over and brought me to a halt before I got too close.

'Who the heck do you think you are?' she demanded.

Big Ben wiped the liquid from his face and looked up. 'Do I know you?'

I heard her take a sharp intake of breath. The rest of the room had turned to watch, all conversation paused to enjoy the scene. 'You... you utter... how could you treat me like this? We had sex less than three hours ago and now you are in here chatting up another woman. Will you not remember her name either?'

138

'Claudia?' he hazarded.

'Yes!' she shrieked in response. 'You said you would call me.'

'Babe, I have honestly never said those words to a woman in my entire life.' He held up a finger to beg a moment's pause as he turned his head to the juicy cherry. 'This won't take a minute, babe. Big Ben will be all yours soon.' Then he locked eyes with the two other women sat at his table and said with a wink, 'And yours too.'

'Oh, my God. You are such a pig,' raged Claudia. Behind Big Ben the three women got up and left.

'Okay, I didn't recognise you, but in my defence, you were facing the other way most of the time.' He delivered the line coolly, but it just added fuel to the fire. Her jaw fell and her cheeks flushed as the crowd tittered. Then she shut her mouth, spun on a heel and stormed off. It was then, as Big Ben inspected his drenched white shirt that Gils stepped in.

'Alright, you. Get out!' he spat. Big Ben didn't react at all to start with, he just sort of wafted a hand in the air as if warding off an annoying fly. Gils was clenching his fists. He was already angry; it had been his starting emotion but it was visibly cranking upwards toward uncontrolled rage. He was a big man and probably not used to being defied, especially not in his family's hotel. He leaned down to get in Big Ben's face. I saw the error he was making but opted to let the scene play out. 'Didn't you hear me? I said get out.'

Big Ben's right arm whipped out to loop around Gils's neck. Gils was overbalanced, his head and chest forward of his feet, so a gentle tug from Big Ben was all it would take to send him flying to the floor.

Big Ben didn't use a gentle tug.

The heir to the family sprawled across the carpet in an untidy mess at Big Ben's feet. Big Ben stayed in his seat, but any advantage Gils might have had was long gone. Nonchalantly, Big Ben placed a foot on the other man's back to hold him in place.

'Am I going to have any more trouble from you, Gils?' he asked. 'I would really rather avoid any further interaction with you.' Gils tried to get up but found Big Ben was able to hold him in place. He fought it for a second before accepting he was stuck. In his chair, Big Ben picked at something invisible under a fingernail as he said, 'I'm not letting you up until I am sure you will behave in a calm manner.' This was unusual behaviour. Normally he would let an opponent get up so he could knock him down again. Maybe he had learned something from me.

'I promise,' hissed Gils through gritted teeth.

Big Ben lifted his foot and picked up a cocktail menu from the table to show how disinterested he was in what Gils might do next. Embarrassed, Gils all but ran from the bar. I doubted the battle was over though. Gils did not strike me as someone that would let such an insult lie.

When he was gone, Big Ben finally looked up. 'I found us a table,' he grinned.

As the marrieds came toward us with drinks balanced on a tray, I excused myself. I was eager to find the way down to the cold store, I had a feeling we might be asked to leave in a more official manner soon, but I was also curious to see where Gils was going. If he was off to grab some staff to oust us, then I wanted to know in advance. Jagjit was here on his Honeymoon, I didn't want him going home with a black eye and it would be wrong to expose any of them to unpleasantness while they were trying to help me.

Gils had vanished down a corridor that led off the hotel's lobby area when he fled the bar, but his general direction was all I knew. Trying to be inconspicuous without looking like that was my intention, I pushed through a door at the end of the corridor as if I belonged on the other side of it, portraying confidence in my whereabouts even though I had none. The door led to a set of stairs going down. They were concrete and in stark contrast to the rest of the plush hotel: I was in a maintenance area of some kind.

'Where are you going?' asked a voice by my ear. It was a good thing I hadn't drunk much liquid yet because I probably would have wet myself. I had been so focused on looking like I was meant to be where I was, that I hadn't looked around to see if I was being followed. As I sagged against the wall, waiting for my heart to recover, I saw that it was Alice behind me. 'I thought you were heading to the toilets so I followed you. Where are we?'

'I have no idea,' I whispered. 'I followed Gils.'

'Is that the tall man that Big Ben just messed with?'

'Yes. His father owns this hotel. I was concerned that he might be off to get some friends to throw us out. Now I am curious about what he is doing down here so I'm going to take a look.'

'Oh,' said Alice. 'Shall I wait here?'

I took a couple of steps down the concrete stairs then glanced back up. 'Up to you entirely. I'm going though.' I wanted to tell Alice to head back to the bar where the chance of getting caught sneaking around the basement of a hotel wasn't so likely, but she was independent and fiery and far more likely to come with me if I told her not to. She came anyway, letting me get a few yards away before she made her decision and caught up.

I motioned for her to be stealthy as we crept along the corridor at the bottom of the stairs to another door. I listened at it for a second with my hand on the handle. Muffled voices were just about audible. Opening the door was risky, I had no idea if I would find a small room with people on the other side or a large space where we could sneak in and listen. There was only one way to find out, so I slowly turned the handle to peek inside.

I had found the underground garage. There were cars in front of me and the cold store was supposed to be in here somewhere. Finding it now would be helpful later when I came back to check out the bodies. The voices were clearer now though, they were speaking French and doing so too fast for me to be able to hear what was being said.

In the underground space, the voices were echoing and hard to pinpoint. They were not in sight though, so I continued forward, sticking to the wall and sidling around the cars to a corner where I stopped and peeked again. I could see Gils. He was facing away from me, his height making him easy to distinguish. Going beyond the corner would expose us, but Alice, being a head shorter than me, slipped beneath my arm to peek as well.

'Who's the girl?' she asked, her question whispered.

The other voice in the conversation was indeed a woman. She wasn't visible but it sounded like Priscille Peran to me. They were in the cold store, or at least that was what I thought I was seeing. There was a pair of silver doors in the wall on the other side of the underground space, both were open. Gils was standing dead centre to them and about a foot inside.

The woman was speaking. I nudged Alice. 'Are you getting any of this?'

She nodded, listening. When there was a brief pause, she started translating, 'She's happy about something. Jubilant. She keeps saying, "I always knew I would win." Any idea what that means?'

It would help if I could see who was talking. I wondered if I could crawl along the floor to get closer, to get a better angle from which to see. I whispered, 'Stay here a second,' as I crouched down. There was too much echo though, as I moved across the concrete, the noise I made sounded deafening to me and I stopped. Glancing back at Alice, I saw how wide her eyes were. Then she darted back behind the corner as footsteps from the cold store and a creak from a hinge reached my ears to tell me the doors were being shut.

They were leaving!

I was crouched behind a car and probably invisible as long as I stayed still, but Alice was going to be spotted the second they turned toward the corridor. What was the right move here? Did I jump up and pretend I had been fishing around for a dropped cufflink? They would see me and ask what I was doing and might be suspicious of my presence, but what could they actually do?

I made the choice and bunched my muscles to get up. As I did so, I looked under the car and saw their feet. They were not coming toward the corridor where Alice was hidden. Instead, they were going away from her. They were still jabbering away excitedly as they went. The tone of the exchange was that of an argument; they were disagreeing about something in passionate terms. Then I heard my name and sound of the woman spitting followed by a door shutting and the space we were in was once again silent.

I held my breath and watched to make sure they had left, maintaining the semi-press up position I had found myself in rather than move again. Behind me, I heard Alice breathe an audible sigh of relief.

As I got to my feet, she said, 'I thought I was busted then.'

'Me too,' I agreed. 'What were they talking about? I couldn't keep up they were talking so fast.' I wondered if Alice might now want to escape back her husband and the safety of the bar, but she showed no sign, so I started walking toward the cold store as she answered.

'I think we came in halfway through a conversation because I could understand what they were saying but not the context of it. The girl was arguing with Gils because she had done something he hadn't wanted her to do. She claimed it was necessary and said he should be glad. What do you think they were talking about?'

I glanced at her. 'I think they were talking about the two dead boys.' We had crossed the room and were standing in front of the cold store doors. 'I'm going to open these now,' I said as I placed my hands on the handles. 'Are you sure you want to see?'

She bit her lip in thought. 'I think maybe I'll just hang around back here.'

'Can you watch for anyone coming?' I asked, which ensured she turned around to face the other way and reduced the chance of seeing what was inside. Once she was facing the other way, I pulled both doors open. Immediately inside the doors was the sled they had been brought down the mountain on and over the bodies was a pair of blankets. As I knelt to expose them, I asked Alice, 'What else did they say?'

'Oh, yes. They went on to talk about having to do something tomorrow. He was still angry about whatever it was she had done and

144

was arguing that they needed to stick with the original plan, but she insisted that tomorrow morning was the perfect opportunity and said something about your interference demanding they accelerate the plan. She sounded quite upset about your presence here and said something about her father. She used a bad word when she said father.'

I filed the information away to consider later and peeled back the blanket to look at the first victim. I couldn't tell which man was which, but I took a photograph of his damaged face so I could identify him later. He was stiff as a board from rigor, but I could get to his wrists by forcing his clothing up. The rope burns on his wrists where he had been tied were clearly that. I had to guess that he and his friend had been snatched, maybe drugged, but definitely tied up and fed to the Yeti. Had they been awake for the attack? Whether they had or not, I was dealing with a ruthless murderer.

I took another series of photographs then undid his coat and underlayers to expose as much of his chest as I could. There was no damage to the skin underneath his clothing that I could see other than those wounds that correlated with the slashes in his clothing. I performed the same inspection on the next man. The rigor prevented me from doing much, but the coroner would be able to perform a full exam when they finally got the cable car working and could deliver the bodies. For now, though, I had confirmed my suspicions: the two young men were murdered.

'We should get back to the others,' I suggested to Alice as I straightened their clothing and covered them over once more. A vigorous nod of her head indicated her agreement, then I realised that she was cold. She had removed her coat when she came into the bar and had been heading to the toilets when she followed me. My breath was coming out in clouds and it had to be below zero in the unheated parking area. I was wearing a jacket and shirt, the jacket of which I now shed to put around her shoulders. It swamped her slight frame, but it was already warm from my body and would help.

With my mind whirling around all the different clues I had to sift, I grabbed the cold store doors. The immediate task was to get out of here without being seen and deliver Alice back to her husband but as I swung the doors shut a small piece of paper drifted across the floor caught in the movement of air.

Seeing my interest, Alice bent to pick it up. 'It's just a receipt,' she said. Then, still staring at it she said, 'Oh.'

We still needed to get back to the others before they sent out a search party so closed the doors and made sure they were shut, then ushered her back the way we had come. On the way I asked, 'Oh what?'

'The name of the business is Dr Monnoglavche chirurgie plastique. This is a receipt for someone to have plastic surgery done. Do you think that was Priscille, the girl you said had her face destroyed?'

'It might have been.' I took the receipt as Alice passed it to me and slipped it into a pocket to consider later.

'I remembered something else,' Alice said once she had a stiff drink inside her and was nursing her second, 'The woman mentioned something about a favourite spot and that was where he would be taken. Does that mean anything?' Alice had her shoes off and was curled in next to Jagjit with her feet tucked under her legs and her husband's arm around her protectively. Dozer was on her lap, adding his warmth to thaw her out while she scratched his chin.

Jagjit had been a little bit panicked when we returned. His wife had been popping to the ladies room and had then vanished for twenty minutes in a resort where there was either a nine-foot killing beast on the loose or a murderer or both.

All eyes were on me as the group waited for me to provide an answer to Alice's conundrum. 'It would help if I knew who the woman was for certain.'

'Who do you think it was?' asked Big Ben.

'It sounded like Priscille Peran.'

'The girl that got injured in the first attack?' he confirmed.

'Yes. I only had one conversation with her though, so I couldn't swear it was her and all I saw was her feet. I would also like to know what it is they have planned for tomorrow morning. Alice made it sound like it was the culmination of something they have been working toward. I just don't know what yet or who it is they are targeting.' I turned my attention toward Alice. 'You said she mentioned her father and was upset with him.'

'Yes. I am ninety-nine percent certain that's what I heard.'

'Ninety-nine percent,' I echoed, 'That's good enough for me.'

'Why? What does it mean?' asked Jagjit.

'It means I am mistaken about the woman. It couldn't have been Priscille because her parents are both dead.'

'So, what's the next step?' Big Ben was giving me his encouraging tone. His attention wasn't really on me though. Having scared the ladies away earlier to ensure they didn't get caught up in Gils violent display, he was now on the hunt for someone new to target, preferably a lady or ladies that had entered the bar after the event I was sure.

I answered the question anyway, 'I will be up early tomorrow to check out some places where I think the Yeti might be. I have a theory that...' I paused because I realised our conversation could be overheard and leaned in so the others knew to lean in also. Then I spoke quietly, 'The Yeti is a polar bear, right? So, someone has messed with it and added the tusks and horns.'

'I thought you had no proof of that,' said Anthea.

'I don't. It is the premise I am going with though. I think we have a polar bear that someone has performed surgery on, and that same person has the ability to control it.'

'How do you control a six-hundred-pound carnivore?' Jagjit wanted to know.

I smiled wryly. 'Actually, the weight is probably nearer one thousand pounds and they can weigh more than that. That's the weight I am using to calculate the dose of tranquiliser I need to administer though. To answer your question: I don't know, but I have seen the dancing bears they have in Eastern European countries and they are controlled by pain. I

148

hate the thought of it, but I found tracks in the snow where the two men had been killed and I think someone is moving it around in a trailer of some kind. The Carons and the Chevaliers both own property in the form of machine rooms for the ski-lifts and on-slope med stations, that sort of thing. If I have this right, then the creature, polar bear or not, is being kept in one of those buildings. I'm going to try to find it before they can kill anyone else and before that nutter Vermont can cleave its head off or get himself killed.'

'What then?' This time it was Big Ben that asked the question. 'What do you do once you have found the Yeti and tranquilised it?'

I shrugged my eyebrows. 'No idea. Gils and the woman he was with tonight have something planned for tomorrow morning though. If it involves the Yeti, I can thwart their plan and with it tranquilised, I can show people what it is.'

'You can't be everywhere though,' said Hilary. 'If you are going after the Yeti, you cannot be here to tail Gils and see what he is up to.'

'That depends how long it takes me to find the Yeti,' I replied defensively.

'He's right,' said Big Ben. 'Gils might be planning murder and if the Yeti doesn't show, he might do it anyway. We need to cover both bases.'

'Too dangerous,' I replied. 'You are talking about having civilians snooping on a man we suspect to be a murderer. I can't endorse that.'

Hilary locked eyes with me. 'No one is asking you to. The same way that no one invited me to tackle the witch that was going to kill you.'

I opened my mouth to argue, but seeing the faces looking back at me, I shut it again.

Jagjit filled the awkward silence. 'We are all here already. You said it yourself: we might all be in danger. Well, we are going to help you do something about it.' His statement got a chorus of yeahs as he raised his glass and waited for everyone else to raise theirs. Then he lifted his in a salute and said, 'Let's solve a crime.'

Unanimously, everyone then decided an early night was called for, although from the look Jagjit was giving Alice, I wasn't sure how much sleep they were going to get. For that matter, Big Ben wanted an early night but was still in search of a companion or companions, so after Jagjit's toast, as everyone emptied their drinks, he surveyed the crowded tables in the bar and left us to zero in on his latest victim.

The rest of us headed back to our hotel, the bright lights of the street and the staff standing lookout at least giving a sense of safety from the Yeti. Despite their best efforts, there were very few people outside and the smaller bars and restaurants beyond the two hotels looked empty.

In my room, the dogs, knowing it was bedtime, scampered to the table on which their biscuit tin sat and waited for their human butler to serve them. As they crunched their treats, I kicked off my shoes and rubbed my feet. I was ready for bed, but I couldn't stop thinking about the receipt I found earlier.

Slipping it from my pocket, I powered up the laptop and poured some water to sip. I had to enter the strangely spelt French word three times before I got it right but found their website instantly. The more I thought about it, the more I convinced myself that it had been Priscille I had heard speaking outside the cold store. It aligned with the plastic surgery receipt too. Checking the website though, it wasn't a company that dealt with disfiguring injuries and reconstructions, not that I could see. Their offerings were vanity procedures such as rhinoplasty and liposuction.

Making an entry in my notebook, I admitted that I had a lot of clues that just didn't make sense.

Yet. Just before I turned in, I sent an email to Jane asking her to check out the plastic surgery business and see if she could find out who owned the credit card that matched the receipt. It was a long shot because only a portion of the number was displayed but I sent her a picture of it anyway. She had pulled off more improbable tasks.

Realisation. Friday, December 2nd 0700hrs

By 0700hrs I had been up long enough to walk the dogs and get some breakfast and now I was heading back to the underground parking garage to snag myself a Ski-Doo. In my pocket was a map of the mountain range on which I had marked the grid references for the buildings dotted about the mountain. If I was right, one of them contained the fake Yeti.

It had been late enough last night that the research request I sent Jane last night hadn't received an immediate response. Instead, I awoke to an apology because she had been out with her boyfriend at the cinema and hadn't seen the email from me until after I had fallen asleep. I should have joined the dots to ask the question earlier, but I felt certain my assistant would be on the task any time now and could picture her wearing Hello Kitty pyjamas and sipping coffee at her breakfast bar while she found the information I needed.

'Good morning,' called a voice as I entered the garage. I wasn't the only one up at this time; Hubert was over by the Ski-Doos I was heading for. He wasn't dressed for going outside, but he looked to be inspecting one of the machines, its seat up to reveal the engine and fuel tank beneath.

'Good morning, Hubert. Are you going out?' I asked as I reached him.

He didn't look up. He had the oil dipstick in his right hand and a rag in the other; checking the oil. 'Not yet,' he said with a shrug. 'Later though. Today is my daughter's funeral. You knew that of course, but we are going out on to the mountain for the service and my wife and I are going skiing this morning. With the ski-lifts down, I suggested we skip that element, but Elizabeth insisted we keep with the plan. To honour Marie, you know.'

I nodded my understanding, not that I really could understand what it was like to lose a child, but I kept quiet because he was sharing, and I would learn nothing if I was talking.

'I just wish we hadn't been on such poor terms when she went out that morning. Regret is such a terrible burden to carry, Mr Michaels. You don't have children, do you?'

'No. That is a privilege I am yet to receive.'

'Then, take some advice from an old man. Don't argue with them too much and never let them walk away after an argument.'

'Can I ask what you were arguing about?'

Gerard sighed the sigh of a tired man, his shoulders slumped and defeated. 'I found out she was dating Gils Chevalier and I forbade her to ever see him again. Can you believe that?' He asked the question with a half attempt at a rueful grin. 'I had so much hate for that family that I was prepared to make my daughter unhappy rather than attempt to offer an olive branch. She told me she loved him, and I threatened to disown her.' It was Gils she was in love with, not Priscille. My wonder over Priscille's comments on Wednesday now answered in part. 'I am a hateful old man, Mr Michaels, unworthy of my daughter's love. My wife was already becoming distant before Marie was... before Monday.'

The door from the hotel opened behind me and I turned to see Big Ben approaching.

'I thought I might find you here,' he said. 'You were trying to go at this thing alone, weren't you?'

I shrugged. 'I was just going to try to find it. I wouldn't have tried to deal with it by myself.'

Hubert's brow furrowed. 'You boys aren't planning to go up the mountain, are you?'

How much should I tell Hubert? He was my client, but he wouldn't be the first client to have lied to me and be leading me into a trap. Was he responsible for the deaths? For the creature's presence here? Then, before I could consider those questions, a thought occurred to me. 'You said you were going skiing this morning. Just you and your wife. Where are you going?'

'The Augille du Rigardi run on the north face. It was Marie's favourite spot.'

I had been adding together dots in my head until he said those words, then my head snapped up as a big piece of the puzzle clicked into place. Marie's favourite spot. Gils and the woman from last night were planning something at a favourite spot. I had to check something. I turned to go, then remembered myself. 'Hubert, I need to borrow a couple of Ski-Doos.'

He wafted a hand in the general direction of the keys, 'Help yourself, boys.'

Hubert was distracted by thoughts of the day ahead; I wasn't even sure he heard me say thank you. 'Ben, can you set up the Ski-Doos? I have to check on something.'

I was already heading back to my room when he replied.

I bumped into Jagjit and Alice as I ran up the stairs two at a time. 'What are you two doing up this early? Shouldn't you be enjoying your honeymoon?'

It was Alice that answered, 'I want to help out. What you were saying last night, Gils knows who you are and will definitely recognise Big Ben

154

but Jagjit and I can probably follow him this morning and see what he is up to.' I didn't respond immediately, so Alice pressed on, 'We are just going to grab some breakfast and then head over to his hotel to see if we can spot him.'

I needed to check my laptop and I needed to call Jane and pick her brains some more. Would Jagjit and Alice get into trouble if they tried to follow Gils? Probably. Would they abandon this course of action if I advocated against it? Probably not.

I said, 'Sure. Good luck. Don't follow him up the mountain though, okay? And stay in contact. Check your phones and watch for messages.'

They both agreed but I was already bounding up the stairs. The dogs jumped off the bed and ran barking at the intruder in their room until I spoke. I had flown through the door and startled them, but they calmed quickly, switching tactics to ask for a treat as if I had been gone for hours. I didn't feel I had time to argue, so I tossed them a gravy bone each and jabbed the power button to boot my computer into life. Then I thumbed the phone button to dial Jane and set it to speaker as I scrolled my finger across the mouse pad.

It was a groggy, sleep deprived voice that answered the phone, 'Hello?'

'Jane?' I asked tentatively.

'Um, yeah, I suppose. I haven't decided yet, but yeah, let's go with Jane.' It was the strangest thing about my assistant; he/she woke each morning gender neutral, maybe that should be; it woke each morning gender neutral? The pronouns were complex enough, I decided, without adding in another level of confusion. Anyway, my assistant got up each morning and only then decided whether to put on boy underwear or girl underwear.

'I need something fast. Can you help?' I had no right to drag Jane from bed this early, but we worked in a business where normal hours were not really a thing and I believed that she bought into the concept as much as Amanda and I did. We had only worked together for a few weeks really, but I was going to have to do something in her wage packet to reflect the additional work she was doing and the value she was adding. Maybe a Christmas bonus would balance the scales? I could think about it later.

'I'm awake,' she said, still sounding like it was only barely true. 'The computer is running, what do you need?' In the background I heard another voice, her boyfriend probably. His deep rumble preceded Jane asking for coffee.

I pressed on. 'This is going to be obscure; I think. Even for me. Can you search for circus acts or freak show acts that involve a polar bear? Not just any polar bear though, one that has been surgically altered to have tusks in its mouth and horns on its head?'

I think it spoke volumes about the general level of weirdness my business handled, that Jane didn't even question my request. While she was doing that, I navigated to a file she had already sent me this week. The one with Marie's school picture in.

'Found it,' said Jane around a yawn. I glanced at the clock in the bottom corner of the laptop screen. About nine seconds had elapsed.

'You're kidding. How on earth did you find that so quickly?'

'I'm brilliant,' she replied deadpan. 'Anything else?'

'I need to see what you are seeing, but otherwise, no I don't think so. Oh, hold on, I sent you an email with a picture last night. Can you see what you can do?'

'A receipt?' she confirmed. 'You just want to know who the card is registered to?'

'Yes, please.'

'That should be easy enough. Give me a little while, okay?'

'Sure, but look, I feel like a slave driver calling you this early in the day. Get this done and have the rest of the day off.' Worry that I was a tough boss was a genuine concern.

'I wish I could. I have work to do, boss.'

My laptop beeped with an incoming email, attached to which was a file containing pictures and a couple of articles clipped from websites. Before I opened them, I opened the picture of Marie's class and asked Jane a question, 'What is it you have to do, that you cannot take a buckshee day off? Amanda and I are here, Amanda doesn't have a live case and I doubt I will need you again today. Take it easy and have a long weekend. I expect Amanda and I will be back on Monday.'

'Yeah,' she drawled slowly, then said, 'Tempest, I have been taking cases as well.'

'Huh?'

'I said...'

'Yeah, I heard what you said, I just had no idea.' This was news, but it probably shouldn't have been. Amanda and I couldn't keep up with the amount of work coming in and Jane was a smart cookie.

'Is it a problem?' I could tell that Jane was concerned she had crossed a line somewhere.

'Not at all. I'm just surprised you didn't say anything sooner.'

'Well, it's a new thing. It just kind of happened, but there are lots of little cases that crop up when the two of you are engaged elsewhere, so after I dealt with the first one, I figured I would see if I could help out with some others.'

'And you have been charging customers and bringing money into the business and I had no idea because I let you do the books.' Jane said nothing in response, but my attention was elsewhere now; I was looking at the photograph of Marie's class. She was seated in the front of three rows, Priscille was in the next row and second from right looking at them properly for the first time and comparing them, I realised what it was that everyone had missed. I didn't have all the answers, but I was getting close.

'Jane, I have to go. I just want to say that I appreciate all that you do and that we need to talk about your position when I return.'

'Oh, God. Don't fire me, Tempest. I was doing what I thought was right.'

I chuckled, which probably wasn't the right thing to do, but I tried to reassure her. 'Jane, I intend to promote you, not fire you. The conversation next week will be about how our developing business will operate with three detectives instead of two. There will be much to discuss, I am sure. Right now, though, I must go. I think there is about to be another Yeti attack.'

How to Tranquilise a One Ton Carnivore AKA I Like Bruises.
Friday, December 2nd 0742hrs

Back in the underground carpark beneath the Constantine hotel, it wasn't just Big Ben waiting for me, Hilary and Anthea were there too. I had never been inundated with so much help and I wasn't sure I really wanted it. Not least because Anthea tended to be a bit prickly, but I had reservations about having either of them along on a trip when I was planning to find, trap and transport a meat eating, highly-dangerous animal that could kill with a single swipe of a paw.

'Is that the gun?' asked Anthea as I approached them. It was slung across my back and I had a bag in my right hand that contained the drugs.

'It is.'

'I thought you said last night that you hadn't come up with a way to get through the Yeti's skin.'

'That's what I said,' I answered without actually answering. Before they could quiz me any further, I had questions for them. 'Are you sure you want to come on this one? This might be the most dangerous thing I have ever done. If anyone gets injured, we will have to get back here before they can be treated.'

In response, Anthea's face was impassive. 'We'll be fine.' Beside her, Hilary looked like he wanted to agree with my thoughts on the matter, but wasn't brave enough to argue with his wife, or perhaps knew when not to push his luck.

I rolled my eyes and swung my leg over the nearest Ski-Doo as I said, 'I think I know where to find it.'

Big Ben frowned as he fired his machine to life. 'Really? I thought you had no idea and we were going to scour the mountain checking all the places it might be and hoping we got lucky.'

'We were. Now, I think we might not have to. I'll try to explain on the way.' I cranked the throttle on my Ski-Doo, letting it pull me across the concrete to the large exit door which detected a vehicle coming toward it and opened automatically.

I wasn't able to explain on the way of course, the engines made far too much noise for that, but I did fill them in when I stopped my Ski-Doo two hundred yards short of the target. We were at the edge of a forest, the tall and ancient pine trees towering above us as I began walking.

'There's nothing here, Tempest,' pointed out Anthea.

'The building we want is just beyond that rocky formation,' I replied as I pointed in the direction I was going.

Anthea, clearly mystified by my actions had more questions though, 'Why aren't we using the Ski-Doos to get there then?'

It was Big ben that answered though, 'Because we don't want anyone that might be there to hear us coming, including the Yeti.' My old army buddy was used to the concept of a stealthy approach.

Anthea's question might have been answered, but she still wasn't done. 'How is it that you know the Yeti is going to be here then and what innovation did you come up with to get the drugs through the Yeti's skin?' They were fair questions that deserved answers. I was fine with Anthea demanding information, I just wasn't enamoured with the way she liked to ask them.

I turned to walk backwards so I could face her while I explained... and promptly fell over as my foot sank in a hole. I picked myself up and tried again. 'The Yeti is a polar bear that was captured as a cub and subjected to terrible operations to alter its appearance. The tusks and horns were added, and it was raised to be a circus act.'

'That's awful,' she cried. 'Who would do that?'

I knew the answer to that question as well, but I was keeping it quiet for now as we were rounding the rocky outcropping and the building was suddenly before us. It was a squat, brick-built thing but it had power cables running into it and the snow around it had been disturbed recently. It was churned up, the caterpillar tracks of a large Snow Cat machine obvious in the compacted snow.

'Is this the place?' breathed Hilary, his voice showing the trepidation I felt.

'We're about to find out.'

'Who owns the building?' asked Big Ben to which I pointed out the sign set just below the eaves of the roof: Caron Enterprises.

'Surely that means your client is the one behind the attacks.' Anthea had hit the nail on the head, but drawing the obvious conclusion didn't mean it was right.

What I said in reply was, 'I think that is what we are supposed to believe.'

'Who else would have access to the building though? His rivals, the Chevaliers can't use this place, surely?'

I didn't answer her last question though. I had reached the back of the building and now knew that I had guessed right. This building was the closest one to the Augille du Rigardi slope that Hubert said he was going to this morning and the only building in the area that I felt was big enough to house the creature. The presence of a large cage mounted on a trailer, hidden from view between the building and the rocks was sufficient to convince me I had found the Yeti's hiding place. All I had to do now was look inside, but as I turned to look back at the building, I saw Big Ben peering in through a window.

'It's pretty dark in there,' he said looking at me, but when he turned back to look inside again, the window was very suddenly filled with the face of the Yeti as it smashed into the glass and shattered it. The window was two feet square, big enough for the Yeti to shove its angry snout through but smaller than its head so the enraged creature was snapping its teeth at Big Ben but thankfully couldn't get to him. Big Ben had thrown himself out of the way in shock nevertheless, surprise and fear etched on his face.

From the floor, he said, 'I forgot just how big that thing is.'

Hilary offered him a hand to get up, just as the Yeti gave up growling through the broken window and slammed his body weight into the roller door by the cage-sleigh thing. The roller door bowed but held as another deafening roar echoed from within the small building. I wanted to rescue the poor creature, but I had to admit a genuine concern that I might not be able to do so safely. The Yeti then reinforced my concern when it slammed into the roller door again. This time it left a dent. A thousand pounds of polar bear was going to come through that door sooner or later and we would need to be somewhere else when it did.

How on earth were they able to control it? Somehow, the trainer/owner was getting it to go in and out of a cage so it could be transported. Thinking about it wasn't going to stop the Yeti from smashing its way out and eating me though. I needed to act.

'Tempest, where's that gun?' yelled Big Ben. His back was flat to the wall by the broken window as he peeked in. 'That thing is going to bust down that door if we don't tranquilise it.'

Anthea ran over to help me get it off my back where the makeshift strap had tangled with the hood of my coat. 'Here,' she said as she freed it. 'Where are the darts?'

'Yeah. About the darts.'

'What about the darts?' she demanded. Both Hilary and Big Ben turned their heads to hear my answer.

'Well, it's about the number of them that we have,' I replied as I knelt in the snow to rummage in the bag.

'Why? How many are there?' asked Hilary.

'There's only one, isn't there? said Big Ben. 'You could only make one so we have one shot at this and have to get it right the first time.'

Anthea put her hands to her face. 'Oh, my God. I knew you would get us all killed. You only have one dart?'

'No, no. Not one.'

'Thank goodness,' she exhaled.

'I don't have any.'

There was a stunned silence as Big Ben, Hilary and Anthea all stared at me. I grinned since I couldn't think of anything else to do. Then the Yeti slammed into the roller door again and Big Ben shouted, 'It's just broken the door. I can see daylight through it now.'

I reached into the bag, pulling out what I did have. The problem with making a dart was that it required a complex mechanism that would force the fluid in the syringe out only once the needle had penetrated the target. I just didn't have the components or the tools to make such a device. After hours of scratching my head I had accepted that I couldn't solve the problem and had approached it from a different angle.

In my hand, I held a clear plastic bag filled with condoms. Inside the condoms, which were tied at the top with a knot, was the drugs which I carefully measured out using my eyeball and luck. The condoms were strong enough that they flew without exploding but would break on impact. All I had to do now was convince it to swallow the medicine like a good little Yeti.

Big Ben's eye flared. 'You are going to feed it those aren't you?' he asked, his voice incredulous.

'Yup.'

'Cool. For a moment there I thought you were going to have something difficult to do.' He turned his head to shout through the window, 'Hey, snow beast. Here beasty, beasty, beasty.'

'Insane,' murmured Anthea. 'You're both mad.'

The Yeti had stopped smashing against the roller door, but two seconds later, it was back at the window. This time though, when it smashed into the wall, the brickwork shifted. Fine dust settled on the snow below as cracks appeared all over the area of wall around the window.

Big Ben uttered a rude word. I had to agree with his thoughts on the matter though. We were going to run out of time really soon if I didn't get the drugs into the beast now.

164

'Ben, get behind me and help me line the weapon up.' He rushed to comply. 'Hilary, I need you to take Ben's place and call for it to attack the window.'

'WHAT!' shouted Anthea, but her husband was already moving.

I lined up the gun on the window. 'We need it to open its mouth,' I shouted. I was going to fire the drugs straight down its throat.

It slammed into the wall again, the brickwork shaking again as more of it moved. It wasn't going to take much more effort from the Yeti to break its way out now. It roared but I couldn't get a clear shot because it was moving too much.

Hilary saw the problem, and stupidly brave as I knew him to be, he offered the Yeti his arm to bite. He just stepped toward the window and thrust his arm toward the hole. I opened my mouth to scream for him to get clear but then the Yeti charged and I saw my chance. From the shadows of the building, into which it kept disappearing, it darted forward to fill the window with its giant mouth as it tried to bite the arm it could see. Hilary threw himself out of the way.

I pulled the trigger.

The condom hit the creature square on its tonsils and burst open, the liquid hitting the soft flesh of its mouth and disappearing down its throat. The Yeti's snarl choked off but it was not able to change its trajectory, smashing into the wall once more and this time breaking through it.

The window flew out, striking Big Ben and me as we were stood right in front of it. Bricks tumbled to the snow as the giant beast continued to smash its way out. The hole it had made wasn't big enough for it to fit through. Not yet, but it was tearing at the bricks with its dinner-plate sized paws and would be free soon.

I backed away, herding Big Ben as I went. Hilary had already scrambled across the snow, Anthea with him as they hurried back to the Ski-Doos. Their efforts would be futile if the Yeti got out though. It would cross the snow far faster than a human and the Ski-Doos were two hundred yards away. Big Ben and I realised that at the same time and stopped our retreat. Better to face it together and hope we could evade it until Anthea and Hilary could grab the Ski-Doos and maybe rescue us.

'I have to admit, I have never fought anything that big before,' said Big Ben. 'But, one swift kick in the nuts though ought to account for it just like anyone else.'

'That's assuming it has nuts.'

'I tell you what,' Big Ben said as the Yeti broke off another chunk of wall, 'you hold it and I'll hit it.'

I smiled despite the desperate situation. We were in trouble this time and I wasn't sure we could both get out of it in one piece. Another piece of wall went, but this time when the creature roared, it also shook its head. It looked like it was confused about something.

The drugs were kicking in!

Big Ben nudged me. 'Do we run?'

'Yeah, I think maybe we do. It's going to run out of steam soon, lets give it some distance to travel.'

Running in deep snow isn't the easiest thing to do though. What we could achieve was a hurried shuffle. Hilary and Anthea were safe though. They were almost halfway back to the Ski-Doos, so if the Yeti didn't pass out before it got to us, they could escape while it was chewing our faces off.

166

I didn't look back when I heard more bricks falling onto the bricks already on the ground, but I did look back a few seconds later when I realised I couldn't hear anything else.

The Yeti was down. It was laying on its front just beyond the fallen masonry and didn't look like it was getting back up. It wasn't unconscious yet; its eyes were open and it was moving its head about a bit. We had done it though, and the new hole in the side of the building had given me a great idea.

Now that the Yeti was incapacitated and we could get close enough to inspect it, I could see that it was a polar bear beneath the tusks and horns. The face had been altered to add brow ridges that changed the shape of the face and made it look more fearsome and the tusk and horns had been surgically added, grafted to its skull and jaw at some point. It made me angry that this creature had been subjected to such poor treatment so that people could make money.

Anthea and Hilary were continuing on to the Ski-Doos. Big Ben had shouted the message so they were going to get the machines and bring them to us. Now he and I were trying to work out which of us was brave enough to check the creature was unconscious and safe to touch. It was huge. So big in fact that I had to believe the one-thousand-pound estimate was on the low side. I had added in a fudge factor when I was calculating how much drug I would need to knock it out, but my math was shaky when it came to estimating how long it might be asleep.

We needed to move it, that much was certain and it had started to snow; thick, white flakes gently settling all around us like a promise.

'Where are we going to take it?' Big Ben asked.

'To Harvarti.'

He eyed me quizzically. 'You want to take the giant beast to the village?'

'Yup.' Then I explained my plan. Hilary and Anthea arrived riding a Ski-Doo each and I explained it again to them.

As usual, Anthea had some questions, but to be fair, my plan wasn't without holes. 'Will it be unconscious for that long?'

'I really don't know. If it wakes up, we can cut it loose though.'

Hilary said, 'That sounds risky. If it gets loose, it could roam anywhere.'

I nodded. 'The dose I gave it should be good for a couple of hours. Ben found some rope in the building so I say we get to it and get moving. Once people know what it is, they will be able to relax. The Yeti threat will be neutralised so they can reopen the mountain and we can find people to do something about this poor creature.'

Everyone nodded; however, it was with reluctance that we began to hogtie the polar bear. The climbers ropes Big Ben had found had to be part of a mountain rescue kit because they were brand new and there was plenty of them. Let me tell you though that lifting a polar bear's leg to pass a rope beneath it is not an easy task. We used up fifteen minutes tying its legs and arms and muzzle but now, if it did wake up, I was fairly certain it would not be able to break free and bring havoc to the community. It felt cruel but it was still the most humane thing I could do.

With ropes from the bear tied to the back of the Ski-Doos, Anthea and I pulled away from the building towing the bear across the slope while Hilary was attached behind as an anchor in case the bear's mass built up speed. Between us, we tentatively headed back to the resort.

It took a while to get there, but we were spotted before we reached the outskirts. Windows facing the mountain undoubtedly allowing anyone looking in our direction to see what we were towing. By the time we were halfway through the small resort, people were spilling from the buildings to see the spectacle and when the first person cheered, it started a ripple that spread through the crowd as it grew.

I turned in my seat to indicate to Hilary that we were stopping, then eased off the throttle to let the machine come to rest. The poor bear was still out cold, something I was thankful for, but I wanted a veterinarian to check it over as soon as one could get here.

I went to check the pulse in the bear's neck, an act that drew a collective gasp from the crowd as they realised we hadn't killed it. They still thought it was a Yeti and were keeping their distance. But despite the reluctance to get too close, the circle around us was closing as people at the back tried to get a look and forced the ones in front of them forward.

An insistent voice cut above the general din of noise as Francois the police chief forced his way through. 'Move aside, I said. Make way.'

When he got to the leading edge of people and separated himself from them, I crossed the distance to him. 'Francois, I need somewhere secure to put the bear and I need a veterinarian to look after him.'

'Hold on, you said bear.'

'Yes, it's a long and complicated story and we need to get to the wake. Suffice to say that this is not a Yeti. It never was, but it is responsible for killing several people at the hands of its owner.'

'Its owner?'

'All in good time, Francois. Will you help me?'

'Of course, I don't know where we can put it though. It's just so big.'

'Do you have a fenced area where we can keep people away from it? It will have to be transported down the mountain over land. It's too unwieldy to get into the cable car and we are too high for a helicopter so we will have to get it far enough down for a heli-lift I guess.'

'There's a lock up for the Snow Cats at the back of the Imperial. We can take it there,' he suggested.

'Sooner rather than later I think, and you will need to put a guard on it. Is the cable car working yet?' I looked across the side of the mountain where I could see the cable trailing away into the distance. It was too far away to see if it was moving but I thought it was.

'They are still testing it but have reported no damage was found. It should be operational later today.'

Just then, Jagjit and Alice broke through the crowd. 'Tempest,' yelled Jagjit as he screeched to a halt. 'We saw... oh, my God, is that the Yeti?' he squealed as he noticed the enormous white lump behind me.

'You were saying you saw something?' I prompted.

'Yeah, yeah. Oh, my God,' he said as he lost his focus once again, 'that is the scariest thing I have ever seen. Is it dead?'

'No, the tranquiliser worked like a charm. I just don't know how long it will be out for.'

Behind me, Francois was having to shout at several young men that had plucked up some courage and were trying to get selfies next to the Yeti's head.

'Mr Michaels,' he called. 'We need to move it to the compound. Right now.'

I looked around. He was right. I hadn't thought this part of the plan through. Not at all. The Yeti was attracting way too much attention as tourists crept ever closer. Thankfully, the bear chose that moment to twitch. It didn't even move much, but it was sufficient to scare those that were looking. Screams lit the air as the crowd tried to implode. Those nearest the beast were trying to run away, while those at the back were trying to push forward to find out what the excitement was all about.

'Let's move him, shall we?' I said to Anthea and Hilary.

Francois forced a hole in the crowd as Anthea, Hilary and I mounted our Ski-Doos again. As we pulled away, Jagjit called out, 'Hey, where's Big Ben?'

The Funeral. Friday December 2nd 1300hrs

By my reckoning, we had arrived back in Harvarti right about when Hubert and his wife were skiing the slope by Marie's favourite spot. The intended Yeti attack would never happen though and the bad guys, because I liked to think of them as bad guys, would now be all flustered trying to work out where the Yeti was. The snow would have done a good job of covering our tracks so they would have arrived at the building they had stashed it in to find a wall busted down and the beast gone.

They would learn that it had been captured the second they returned to the village, but they would remain calm and confident because they had gone way, way out of their way to cover their tracks, so to speak. They had sewn a trail of misdirection to ensure the blame for the deaths, all of them, would be left at someone else's door. However, I was going to wreck their calm and spoil their day.

Even though it had only been three days, it felt like I had been in this snowy wonderland for weeks. The case had looked impossible two days ago when the man in a suit turned out to be nothing of the sort but once I found the first piece of the puzzle it was like picking at the edge of a piece of Sellotape: once I had prized the first edge up, it got easier and easier until I could grab hold with both hands and yank it free. I didn't know everything yet, but with what Jagjit and Alice had seen while I was up the mountain, I believed I knew enough to close the case.

The wake was being held in the Constantine Hotel in a private function room closed off to guests. A private ceremony for friends and family had been conducted at 1300hrs at the bottom of the Augille du Rigardi. Hubert would ski the run with his wife and arrive at the service while other attendees were being driven there in Snow Cats. I imagined there would be one or two faces at the service that would be thoroughly shocked to see Hubert and his wife arrive unscathed.

Since I was confident the threat to my client had been nullified, I was waiting for the wake itself where I had a couple of special guests to present. With a small amount of time to kill, I had sent invitations to the special guests, with a mild threat enclosed should they choose to not attend. I had also enlisted Francois to escort them to the wake since they were not officially invited. He had been only too happy to help, his curiosity to hear what I had to say almost bubbling over into a demand because he was the police chief and had a right to know, dammit.

The dogs were pleased to see me when I got back to the room and were even more pleased to be allowed to run around outside. It was warm today, the sun trapped between the buildings of the resort reaching a comfortable sixty degrees. They scampered and played and chased each other since there were no birds to scare from their lawn or squirrels on the fence. I walked them around to the enclosure Francois had put the Yeti in, their little noses beginning to twitch long before they could see anything; they could smell something unfamiliar.

I wanted to make sure the bear was being left alone. I didn't like that it was still tied up, but it wouldn't break a sweat escaping the compound, so the bindings were necessary; it was just too dangerous. Thankfully, the poor bear was still unconscious when I got to it. Francois had deputised a couple of hotel staff, big men that looked capable to warding off potential idiots that might try to get close to it. There were people nearby, but all were keeping a respectful distance from the fence. Then I noticed that among the onlookers was Vermont. Stefan and Arthur were elsewhere, the tall American man without them for the first time that I had witnessed.

Bull barked at the sleeping bear. It was his warning bark, the one tinged with promised aggression should it not be heeded. He didn't know that he was the size of a shoe and about as dangerous. Of course, his dopey brother joined in because they are a two-fer; one dog barks, the other will join in purely from a sense of brotherhood. It didn't matter what was being barked at; the point was to bark.

I shushed them, but they had drawn Vermont's attention and he was walking across to speak with me.

'You are a surprisingly resourceful man, Mr Michaels.' I inclined my head to acknowledge his compliment. He was staring wistfully through the fence at the bear. 'I am not used to being wrong and somehow this is twice that I have misjudged the nature of the quarry when I have had dealings with you. I cannot decide if you are very lucky or if I am losing my touch.' He smiled at himself. 'A polar bear. I never would have guessed.' Then he turned away, pausing for a second to make a parting comment over his shoulder, 'Until next time, Tempest Michaels.'

I watched him go, glad that I had got to the creature first, though I had to wonder if Vermont would have got himself killed in his quest to take the bear's head. It was unimportant now. I could see that the bear wasn't being abused and for now, at least, there was nothing more I could do for it. As I started back toward the hotel, I called Big Ben.

'Hey, bro,' he answered.

'Were you successful?' I asked.

'Damned skippy. I'm on my way back now.'

'Top man. I'll see you soon. You know where to find me.'

I disconnected and called Amanda, tapping my foot while I waited for her to answer, but it rang through to her voice mail. Disappointed, I slipped my phone back into a pocket. I would see her soon enough I hoped. They were doing their best to get the cable car working and had lots of reasons why they wanted it operational that far exceeded delivering Tempest's girlfriend.

The dogs continued scampering back and forth searching for something to sniff that wasn't snow. They didn't find much but were enjoying the fresh air and freedom after a morning cooped up in my room. I walked them back to the hotel, got a nod from the lady on reception and a round of applause as people now inside the hotel recognised me from outside. I was the man that had caught the Yeti, even though it was no such thing.

I flipped a mental coin and went to the bar for a coffee. It was lunch time and my breakfast was a long way behind me now. Nervous energy was balling inside me and I probably needed a stiff drink rather than a shot of caffeine that would jack me up even more. When the barman appeared, I ordered the coffee anyway; I needed a clear head for what was to come so for the next thirty minutes, I ran through the facts in my head and ate a sandwich.

When I heard the funeral party returning, I sent a group message to Big Ben and Jagjit and Hilary. I had already asked too much of them in the last couple of days and would need to find a suitable way of rewarding them for their help. Were it not for them, had I come alone, I would most likely have been killed by the Yeti on the first morning.

I gathered my things and roused the dogs from their slumber beneath my table to lead them through to the private lounge set aside for the wake. A sign on the door advised all that a private function was taking place and that attendance was strictly by invitation. I ignored that, slipping inside and finding a large high-backed chair that I placed in the centre of a circle of chairs I formed. It was time to play the part of the ring master.

'What are you doing here, Mr Michaels?' asked Mrs Caron as she came into the room on her husband's arm. 'This room is reserved for my daughter's wake.'

'Is everything alright?' Hubert asked, possibly picking up on the nervous energy I felt.

Others filed into the room behind him, Francois in his uniform, the hotel manager Michel Masson, Priscille Peran being escorted by Gils Chevalier and half a dozen other guests that must be close to the family.

'Please, come in. Take a seat. I'm afraid the time has come to explain what has been happening here.'

Hubert stared at me. 'Mr Michaels, I don't think this is the time. Please leave us to grieve now and I will see you in my office later today.'

'I'm afraid not, Hubert. What I have to say cannot wait. Nor would you want it to.' The stream of people entering the room had stopped and they were all milling around now confused by the unexpected turn of events. I indicated to the chairs. 'Please, this will not take long.'

When no one moved, I added, 'This is to do with what happened to Marie, Hubert. The deaths this week were not accidents, they were murders.'

On using the M word, several heads shot up. Mrs Caron's hand flew to her face in shock. 'What are you saying? Someone murdered my daughter.'

I didn't answer the question but indicated to the chairs again. In stunned silence, Hubert led his wife into the circle and took a seat. She sat next to him as others too claimed chairs. Francois remained at the back of the room, looking immoveable, his handgun visible and exposed on his right hip. With forced calm, I scanned around the faces now looking intently at me then glanced to the back of the room where I could see Jagjit and Hilary lurking.

At my nod they came into the room. 'We have some additional guests,' I announced as Gerard Chevalier strode purposefully into the room.

Hubert reacted as I expected he would: with volcanic eruption. 'What is the meaning of this?' he thundered, getting to his feet even as I stepped in to block his way. 'Chevalier I warned you never to set foot in my hotel.'

'That's because you don't want me to see how run down it is,' Gerard countered.

I put my face in front of Hubert's. 'Sit down.' The tone of my voice was enough to distract him so as he looked at me, I said, 'Please. This is necessary.'

'Why was I summoned, Mr Michaels?' demanded Gerard. 'Who are you to threaten me.'

'I'm the one with the answers, Monsieur Chevalier. You are here because you are concerned I might know more than you think I can. Will you please take a seat?'

Gerard Chevalier didn't move. Not until Francois cleared his throat that is. Then he spun around. 'I've heard enough. You can't keep me here.' But his path was blocked by Francois as the ageing official prevented the younger man from leaving.

'Take a seat please, Gerard, there's a good fellow,' he said.

Grumpily, Gerard gritted his teeth but said nothing as he crossed the room and sat down. He found himself opposite Hubert and his wife, and each party was trying to out stare the other, raw hatred the only emotion showing.

'Thank you for indulging me,' I started. 'I want to start by explaining to everyone how it was that I came to be here. I solve cases where my clients either believe they have something unexplained happening that may have a paranormal explanation, or they are the victim of a hoax designed to hide another crime by making it appear that there is a paranormal explanation. In this case, a creature being passed off as a Yeti was used to kill three people. You all know now that it wasn't a Yeti, yes?' A ripple of nods confirmed that the news of the bear had reached them. I continued, 'Instead the creature trapped outside is a polar bear, captured as a cub and trained through pain to obey its owner. Horns, tusks and other enhancements were added to alter its appearance and it has spent its life as a circus attraction in Russia until it was brought here as part of an elaborate ruse.'

My audience were silent, most of them staring at me in rapt fascination. Not all though, there were one or two that looked nervous now.

I picked up my narrative again. 'I came here to prove that the Yeti was nothing more than a man in a suit and I will admit that it shook me when I came face to face with the bear. I had a lucky escape, as did Priscille, isn't that right Priscille?'

Suddenly in the spotlight, Priscille gulped. She opened her mouth to speak but I waved her to silence.

'I'll come back to that in a little while, Priscille.' She exchanged a glance with Gils and looked at the exit, but she stayed where she was as I started talking again. 'I have a research assistant back in my office in England. She's a little unusual but she is great at finding things out. It didn't take her long to discover that the two men killed by the Yeti during the storm on Wednesday night were involved in a scandal with Marie. There were some unsavoury photographs.' No one said anything, but Mrs Caron buried her face in her hands dramatically and Hubert looked like he was about to get angry at me for bringing the subject up at his daughter's wake. 'Their untimely deaths could have been put down to misadventure, but I found rope burns around their wrists where they had been tied up. They were fed to the bear, you see.'

A sharp intake of breath reverberated around the room.

'They were murdered and I wondered at the time if Hubert might himself be involved.'

'What?' he exclaimed, his shock at being under suspicion almost causing him to rise.

I fixed him with a smile. 'The two men abused and embarrassed your daughter and brought shame to your family. They then had the audacity to stay here, wandering around in plain sight, their presence a permanent reminder of the scandal. No one would blame you for harbouring a grudge, but tell me, was it you or your wife who was most upset and embarrassed?' I locked eyes with him, watching for the tell-tale sign that would tell me if I had guessed right or wrong. I saw it, brief though it was as he quickly glanced at his wife. I continued before he could ask the question I could see forming on his lips. 'There is good news here though, Hubert, although I doubt you will find it pleasing.'

His eyebrows had involuntarily risen with curiosity. 'My research assistant discovered that Marie Caron's credit card was still being used.'

Hubert stared at his wife. 'You said you cancelled it.'

'That it was being used was not nearly as interesting as who was using it.' I paused for effect before finishing with, 'The culprit, was her.' I turned and pointed at Priscille Peran.

'What?' Hubert's reaction came out surprised and angry at the same time.

'It was what the credit card was being used to pay for that solved the case in many ways.' I was facing Priscille now, piercing her with my gaze. 'How bad were the cuts to your face, Priscille? Why don't you take the bandages off and show us?'

'Now see here,' shouted Gils rising to his feet.

I ignored him even though he was now standing between me and Priscille. She looked smaller than ever as she tried to shrink into her seat. 'How about the sunglasses, Priscille? Why don't you take them off, just for a moment? You have brown eyes, right? Not bright blue ones. That is the eye colour Marie had.'

Slowly, and with an unhappy smile, Priscille reached up and removed her sunglasses. Her head was bowed, looking down at the carpet, but everyone in the room was waiting for her to raise her head. As she did so she locked eyes with Hubert and said, 'Hello, Daddy.'

This time the collective gasp was accompanied by squeals of shock and Mrs Caron fainted against her husband's arm.

I focused my attention on her. 'That's a little dramatic, don't you think, Mrs Caron. After all, you falsely identified her body, so you knew she was alive.'

Hubert leaped from his chair causing his wife to spill on the floor. 'What does he mean Elizabeth?' Poor Hubert's head was swinging from his very much alive daughter to his treacherous wife unable to decide which to look at.

'I'm afraid, Monsieur Caron, that you are the intended victim of an elaborate ruse that was intended to end with your death.'

'What?'

'Your daughter faked her own death so that she could operate unimpeded while she plotted against you. She has an appointment at a plastic surgeon in Paris next week where I imagine she plans to have her face altered slightly so that she is not instantly recognisable as Marie Caron. It was when I found a photograph of her graduating class that I realised just how similar Marie and Priscille look. Hair, height, and body shape are all very close. Only her eyes would have given her away but your wife identified your daughter's body and no one questioned her opinion. Marie needed to stay close by to make sure the rest of her plan came to pass but had to hide in plain sight. She was well known in Harvarti having grown up here, where in contrast Priscille was new here and not known by many people.' I turned to face Marie as I said, 'I couldn't work out why you were both so far from the path that day. There was no reason to venture that far into the woods unless you were luring her there to kill her. Did you befriend her with this plan in mind? Or was her family's fall from grace just a happy coincidence that played into your hands?'

Marie replied coolly, 'How is it that I am supposed to have controlled a giant bear, if we are to believe that is what it is?'

'A good question which I shall answer shortly.' I paused and changed tack, 'I overheard you and Gils arguing in the Imperial Hotel's underground parking garage last night. He was upset that you had used the bear to kill Remy and Andre, no doubt claiming that it was unnecessary and brought risk you could do without. You didn't care about that though, did you? Though, of course, you were not alone in your desire for revenge.' I switched my attention back to my client. 'Your wife was the outraged party, was she not?'

'Hubert don't listen to this fool,' Elizabeth Caron demanded. 'He is just spewing nonsense.'

I waited for her to finish before continuing. 'Your wife, I suspect, was the instigator. Whose idea was it for you to ski the Augille du Rigardi this morning, Hubert?' I watched as his face filled with disbelief. 'The Yeti was being kept in the maintenance building under tower nine of the chair lift. Had I not captured it this morning, I believe you would have been led into a trap. You see, I really do hate to burden you with yet more bad news, but your wife is having an affair,' I paused for effect then stuck out an accusing finger, 'with him.'

'Really?' asked Hubert, genuinely sounding nonplussed. 'Jacques from the post office?'

I lifted a single eyebrow and checked my finger to see if the direction I was pointing could possibly be misconstrued. Jacques was in the next row of chairs and his mouth was hanging open in mute horror as the woman next to him, undoubtedly his wife, lined up a fist and whacked him in the face.

'No, no, no. Not him,' I explained taking two paces forward to point again. 'Him.'

This time there was no ambiguity as my finger was all but touching Michel Masson's chest.

'It's a lie,' Mrs Caron screamed.

'Of course, it's a lie,' said Hubert's hotel manager as he rose to his feet. 'I am gay.'

Hubert didn't know which way to look. His face was murderous, and I could see he was struggling to keep himself in check. Sensing the danger, his wife scrambled out of his grasp, crossing the room to reach Michel.

'The gay claim is getting harder to defend, Michel,' I pointed out. Fixing him with a look, I said, 'Your advances, intended no doubt to allay suspicion, had the opposite effect. Big Ben thought there was something off about you from the very start, though I will admit my money was on Gerard Chevalier as Mrs Caron's lover.'

'What?' said Gerard, he was just as thrown as Hubert by the revelations.

'Hubert, I'm afraid a conspiracy was underway to remove you. I thought for a while that your rival Gerard Chevalier was at the centre of it. It was clear the two of you both bore grudges and he stood to gain the most from your demise. It was your daughter though, determined to pursue her relationship with a man you forbade her to see and Gils himself, who, together with your wife believed the Constantine hotel would flourish under new management. She recruited her mother, no doubt the pair of them cooking up the idea for her to seduce Michel because they needed him to hide the transactions that would incriminate you.'

'Err, what?' asked Michel, the question aimed at Elizabeth Caron.

'Perhaps I have that wrong, Michel,' I admitted. 'I cannot prove it unequivocally, but I suspect you were never part of the long-term plan. You will remember that you gave me your key card as part of your fake gay act. Well, this afternoon, while most of us were up the mountain rescuing the bear and most of the people in this room were preparing for the funeral, my resourceful honeymooning friends, Jagjit and Alice were watching what was going on here. One of the things they saw was Mrs Caron letting herself into your room. She had something with her when she went in and she didn't have it when she came out. An hour ago, I quickly searched your room, looking for places that someone might hide something if they didn't want it to be found until the right time.'

The colour was draining from Mrs Caron's face as I unveiled all that I knew.

'Beneath the dressing table drawers, where no one but the police would ever look, is a small bag containing blood-soaked ropes.' Michel Masson's face snapped around to stare at Mrs Caron. 'DNA testing will reveal the blood belongs to the two young men you helped to murder at Mrs Caron's request. Won't it, Elizabeth?'

'You can prove nothing,' she snapped.

With a nod of my head to accept what she said, I opened my mouth to continue but Michel Masson spoke first.

'Why, Elizabeth?' he asked, his voice sounding small and pathetic because he knew he had been duped.

When she didn't speak, I filled in the blanks. 'You were a tool, Michel. You were necessary because she wanted you to distract me. That was why she insisted you pretend to be gay. That is how it happened, isn't it?' I saw the truth of it in his expression. 'Once Hubert was dead though, she would want rid of you. I imagine her plan was to kill you. What's one more body after all? So, the bloody ropes were nothing more than insurance should something go wrong.'

'Why?' cried Hubert, speaking for the first time in minutes, the question clearly aimed at his wife.

'Because you are a fool, Hubert. You have ignored me and neglected your business so you could conduct a campaign of revenge against a man that hadn't done anything to you. When your daughter fell in love with his son, you forbade her from seeing him. *You* gave us no choice.'

'I'm leaving,' announced Marie Caron getting to her feet, Gils rose with her but she didn't get far.

Francois said, 'Sit down, both of you,' his hand hovering near the butt of his pistol as a silent threat.

Gils turned back to me, a haughty and confident grin on his face. 'You can't keep us here. What is it that we are supposed to have done? All I hear is conjecture. What evidence do you have to link this to any us of?'

'I'm so glad you asked.' I turned my head to the door and called loudly, 'Ben.'

The door opened as Big Ben came through it. Dangling from one meaty hand was the Russian bloke from the room next to mine. His face looked like he had resisted Big Ben's request to accompany him and learned that it was unwise to do so.

'Any trouble?' I asked.

He shrugged his giant shoulders, 'Not really.' I had left Big Ben up the mountain to lie in wait for the Russian. When I asked Jane to look for a circus act this morning, she had sent me a flier on which the unmistakeable face of the man next door was emblazoned. It was superimposed in front of the fearsome looking polar bear and above its head was the word йети – which my computer handily translated into Yeti. My confidence that Big Ben would subdue the man and bring him back to Harvarti on whatever transport he had been using, had of course proved accurate, so here he was.

'Ladies and gentlemen, this is Victor Korylenko. He is the man that trained the bear and kept him as a pet until he was recruited by Gils Chevalier and brought here. Hubert, your accounts will show that he has been staying in your hotel and that you have been picking up the tab for his stay. Evidence will also show that the bear was being kept in one of your properties. All of the evidence was meant to point to you so that when you were killed by the Yeti this morning, it would look like the beast you had used to exact revenge on the two boys had turned on its master. I cannot be sure about the rest of it, but I assume that Gils then intended to send Victor and the bear away, the legend of a Yeti in this area would bring in tourists for years and Marie would soon return from surgery as Priscille while he and his father together with your wife and daughter ran the whole resort. Both hotels under one ownership.'

Gerard Chevalier left his seat, he was staring at his son, his disbelief clear. As he backed away from the accused, he found himself standing next to Hubert, the two men exchanging a brief glance before Gerard turned his attention back on his offspring. 'Gils? Is all this true?'

Gils didn't answer though, he hadn't yet sat back down after getting up when Priscille announced she was leaving. I might have got some of the details wrong, but the basic concept of their plot was laid bare. The evidence might point to Hubert's involvement, but it would not take long to prove otherwise. I saw the glint in Gils eyes before he moved, but I was too far away to do anything. From inside his jacket, he produced a gun. Not an old rotary barrel six-shot special like Francois had, but a gleaming new automatic. I couldn't tell what make it was, but branding was an unnecessary detail because I could tell that he was going to use it.

Gils grabbed Marie's hand and yanked her toward the door, lifting the gun and shooting Francois before the older man could even see what was happening. In the enclosed space the blast was deafening and there were more shots coming. As he began running, tiny Marie getting dragged along behind him, he fired shots in the general direction of Victor, then lined his weapon up on Hubert.

More rounds spit from the gun, but I was too far away to save my client. As I watched the scene play out, it was Gerard that barrelled into Hubert, saving him as rounds thumped into the woodwork behind where he had just been standing. Then, except for the screaming, all was quiet. Gils had darted through the door and was gone. There was a scream from outside and the sound of another shot as the fleeing couple made good their escape.

'Are you hurt?' I asked Hubert, my tone insisting a fast response.

'No. No, I don't think so.'

That was good enough for me, I scrambled up and ran across the room, 'Ben? Where are you?' My dogs were running along behind me, excited from the activity they didn't understand.

'Down here.' He was just picking himself up from the floor as well. It looked like he had used his body as a shield to stop them from shooting Victor. Not that he was shot, there was no sign of blood, but smoke was drifting from the hole in the wall near them where a bullet had buried itself. What good killing Victor now might have done I could not imagine. 'I thought I'd had it then,' said Big Ben as he regained his feet. 'Where'd they go?'

'Out this way.' The new voice was Hilary, both he and Jagjit had been hanging around at the back of the room and were now tending to Francois who was sitting with his back to the wall looking at a hole in his chest. He was leaking blood, but the shot had hit low on the ribs on the right-hand side and would not endanger his life.

He chose that moment to look across at me and give me a weak thumbs up. 'You want my gun?' he asked as he unsnapped the clip on his holster.

I grabbed it from him, then Big Ben thumped me on the shoulder. 'Come on, Tempest. Let's go!'

He was right, it was time to chase the bad guys. I couldn't just leave though, there were killers and conspirators in the room I was leaving and I needed to lose the dogs. Jagjit and Hilary went out the door with Big Ben, the three of them disappearing as I scooped the dogs and thrust them at Hubert.

'Take care of them for me, please. I'll be back soon.' I tossed the police chief's gun to Gerard shouting, 'Hold them until help arrives,' as I sprinted after my friends.

I could see Big Ben outside the hotel doors, his height making him easy to spot. Racing to catch up with them, I burst through the doors and into the cooler air outside. None of us had winter coats on but the sun was high in the sky and it was warm enough for now.

'Do you see them?' Jagit asked. They had stopped in the area beyond the doors because they had no idea which way Marie and Gils had gone. Ahead of us the cable car cable was lazily turning but there was no car in sight for them to have tried to escape on. If they wanted to get down the mountain, they were going to have to do it on foot or using a Ski-Doo. I realised how accurate my thoughts were as one burst from the underground garage with Gils driving.

Marie was hanging on to his back as they flew over the snow, the throttle all the way open in his haste to escape. He shot through the far end of the resort heading toward the cable car station. Common sense told me he couldn't possibly escape. He had just shot a cop, and together, he and Marie were responsible for the murder of three people. Even if they could get away from Harvarti, where could they go?

I wasn't leaving it to chance though, I sprinted for the garage, slipping more than once on the snow as the sun melted it. The attendant inside still looked shocked, the keys to the Ski-Doo most likely taken at gunpoint. I didn't have a gun, but I didn't bother asking either. I grabbed keys from the hooks they were hung on and threw them at my friends as they arrived. Matching the numbered key to a machine, I cranked the throttle and left the others in a cloud of smoke. They would catch up or they wouldn't. The important thing was to catch Gils and Marie, but as I shot across the snow in the direction they had gone, I could hear the others following me. I didn't turn to look at them though. At the speed I was going, one mistake might put me in hospital and there were cliffs around that I might not see until it was too late.

Concerned for my safety but pushing the machine anyway, I kept the throttle open. Gils and Marie had left an easy to follow set of tracks in the snow and it didn't take much more than a minute to spot them ahead of me. What at first was a black dot, soon became the shape of a Ski-Doo seen from the back and then I could make out Marie's bandaged head and her hair whipping about in the wind. With two on the machine, they couldn't outrun us.

I glanced back, the others were right on top of me, Big Ben closest which made sense on this downhill run as he was the heaviest. When I looked back in the direction I was going, I could see that Gils and Marie were fighting. Her screams could just about be made out over the noise of the engines, then suddenly she pitched into the snow, thrown from the machine by her lover as he realised he had to lose the excess weight if he wanted to escape.

I didn't slow down for her though, I belted straight by. Big Ben or Jagjit or Hilary would stop for her or none of them would and we could collect her later. It would take her an hour to walk back to the resort and much, much longer to walk anywhere else.

Gils though was getting away from me. The gap, which had been steadily closing since I first spotted them, was now opening up again. I hunkered down over the handlebars to reduce the drag my body was creating but it made no perceivable difference. Suddenly Gils dropped from view as he flew over a drop, then reappeared again as he powered onwards. The terrain until now had been smooth slopes with few obstacles, but we had trees and rocks ahead. I gritted my teeth as I too flew over the bump, the engine freewheeling for a second as I hung in the air before slamming back to earth with a bone-crunching impact. Big Ben flew over the same jump an instant later, he was right on me now and about to overtake.

Ahead, Gils had entered a sparse treeline and was weaving between the trees. Beside me Big Ben was shouting something. I couldn't hear him over the noise of the engine, but I wasn't stopping for anything. Gils vanished from view again, going down another drop no doubt to appear again in a second. If I let off the throttle, he would escape.

Big Ben shouted again. He was right next to me and standing up in his seat to get in my face. Then, before I could yell that I couldn't hear him, he leaped. His shoulder slammed into my arm, tearing me from the machine as we both went tumbling into the snow. End over end I bounced, my momentum carrying me almost to the edge of the jump I had been about to take.

As I came right way up, I saw the Ski-Doo fly into the air and sail to its death. The jump wasn't a jump, it was a cliff. Big Ben had saved my life. I rolled over to check where he was, finding him a few feet behind me, sitting up and nursing his left arm.

A quick check revealed that I was bruised, but otherwise uninjured. I had jarred my neck and my face hurt where it had slammed into the snow. I had no injuries that were worth reporting though. All thanks to Big Ben.

'How you doing over there, buddy?' I asked.

'Better than Gils, I'll bet. Any sign of him?'

I turned around and edged toward the drop off, then peered as far as I could. I didn't want to get too close to the edge, it was snow not rock after all and could choose to fall off at any point. 'I don't see him,' I replied. Rather than stand, I crawled across the snow to get away from the edge and then got to my feet. I offered Big Ben a hand up.

'Tempest?' he said as he clambered to his feet, his left hand still cradled across his body.

'Yeah?'

'How the heck are we going to get back up this mountain?'

Big Ben and I had trudged up the hill for over an hour before we were spotted. Jagjit and Hilary had lost sight of us and had been arguing about whether to go after us or take Marie back to the hotel when actual police had arrived. At some point the cable car had been declared operational and the first people on board were police from Tignes whom Francois had called. Arriving in Harvarti, they had commandeered some Ski-Doos and had come after us. Finding the chaps arguing over Marie, they had taken charge and sent them back to the hotel escorted by a cop. Another cop had handcuffed Marie and taken her back as well.

Big Ben's wrist was probably broken, not that I thought it would slow him down for long if at all, but we would have gladly accepted a ride back to the resort even if we had been in peak fitness. The sun had already set when they found us, and I was a good way beyond cold.

As the police officer I was clinging to, brought the Ski-Doo to a halt, I found that my hands no longer worked properly, we had rushed out into the icy environment ill-prepared for a prolonged exposure and the dipping temperatures the day's end would bring. The cold had penetrated to my core and was threatening hypothermia if I didn't get warm soon.

Our arrival was seen from people inside the hotel though, Hubert Caron and Gerard Chevalier both rushing out to give assistance along with members of hotel staff. They brought blankets and helped us inside where warm air hit my skin like needles dipped in fire. I wanted to ask Hubert and Gerard how it was that they came to be working together now, but my jaw was chattering too much, and my face was numb. I was offered brandy but managed to stutter out, 'Tea, please.' The warmth rising from the cup used first to steam some life into my face before it cooled enough for me to drink it.

193

Finally able to speak, I had answered Hubert and Gerard's questions, of which there were plenty. It started with the most obvious which was from Gerard. I had answered as gently as I could but had to watch as he then wept at the news of his son's death. From the description Big Ben and I gave, they believed he had fallen into a glacier many hundreds of feet below. There was no chance of survival and his body would be hard to find. Hubert expressed that they would try though and had given the other man a brief hug of camaraderie as he did. Somehow, among the treachery and tragedy, the two men had found some common ground. Gerard left us at that point, his grief and confusion too great to air in public.

When he was gone Hubert asked, 'Do you know how Victor was able to control the enormous bear?'

I finished my tea and put the cup back on the table. I was no longer shivering uncontrollably but I was still cold. The hot liquid was helping me, but I would need a long bath or a shower yet. 'I don't,' I admitted. 'There wasn't time to question Victor and he speaks very little English I'm afraid.'

Across the table, Big Ben said, 'He had a little electronic box with a button on it that must have something to do with it. I waited for him to arrive and watched to see if he had a weapon I would need to deal with, but he was shouting in Russian and pressing the button on the box while he looked around for the bear.'

Gerard spoke again, 'Then you might be interested to know that the veterinarian that came up from Tignes found a radio receiver tucked behind the bear's left ear. He believes there is something in the bear's head that gives it an electronic shock.'

'That would force me into submission,' I breathed, horrified by the idea. 'Will it be okay?'

'That I cannot say,' replied Hubert. 'It may be too dangerous to be allowed to live and it certainly cannot be returned to the wild.'

'Where are my dogs?' I asked, suddenly remembering them.

'Oh, um, they are being looked after by the ladies in the spa.'

'I'll get them,' said Big Ben at the mention of women. He had drunk his tea and was on his second brandy, the large balloon glass dwarfed by his hand as he cupped it. Sitting next to him and unnecessarily close, was a member of Hubert's staff, a young woman with a first aid kit who must have had some medical training because she had declared Big Ben's wrist was not broken after all. She was immobilising it nevertheless while trying not to gaze at Big Ben's stupidly pretty face.

'I wasn't sure what to do with them,' Hubert said. 'The police arrived with the coroner to collect the bodies of Remy and Andre but of course they had to forget that task and call for reinforcements. They were all over me with questions so I tucked your dogs in the spa with my wife's dogs.'

I laughed. I bet they had hated that.

Hubert hurried away, returning a minute later being led by my Dachshunds. The pair of them looking very pleased with their afternoon. I was as pleased to see them as they were to see me, and I was warm enough now that I could get up and move so I picked them both up for a fuss. They clambered all over me in their attempts to lick my face and nuzzle my neck. I squeezed them both tight until they wriggled to be set free then plopped them both back on the floor. The police were still milling around and would want to take statements from me soon no doubt. However, I was hungry again and I needed to change my clothes, plus it had been an eventful day and I needed to get clean.

'If the police want me, Hubert, please have them call my room. I need to sort myself out and have some quiet time.'

'Yes. Yes, of course.' He put out his hand for me to shake. 'Mr Michaels, I cannot thank you enough for what you have done. I must confess I feel a bit lost now with my family in custody and accused of murder. How could I have had no idea?'

I couldn't answer that question for him so I just shrugged.

Seeing that he was keeping me, he patted my arm and turned to walk away himself, then turned back. 'I forgot to tell you. Your wife arrived. She was given a spare key to your room.'

'My wife?'

Seeing my confusion, he said, 'She said she was your wife. Amanda Michaels. No?'

A little voice from three feet south sounded a bugle charge. 'Thank you, Hubert. I am glad she was able to get here.' I smiled and left him in the lobby as I hurried to the room.

The Dachshunds scampered around my feet, bouncing off each other as they ran and played, but they got to the door first and instantly started sniffing under the door; they could tell there was someone inside. I searched my pockets for the key card, coming up empty until I remembered it was in the back of my trousers. It had to be a miracle that it was still there.

My heartrate began to rise as I swiped the card, watched the little light change from red to green and pushed the door open. It had only been a couple of days since I last saw her, and it was still the very early days of our relationship, but I couldn't deny the elation I felt at the opportunity to see her. With all that had happened since I arrived, it felt like weeks since we kissed.

There was no one in my room though. The dogs had rushed in but otherwise I was alone. Then I spotted a bag that wasn't mine which had its contents spilled across the bed. Maybe she was in the restaurant. I needed to get a bath and clean myself up before she saw me so perhaps it was best that she wasn't here right now.

I pushed the bathroom door open and stopped dead because there she was. The shower was running, and she had her back to me, her blonde hair a wet mass of soapy bubbles as she shampooed it. Guiltily, I realised I was staring at a naked girl without her permission to do so. I turned my eyes down and began backing out of the room.

Then Bull barked from between my feet, the little dog announcing my Peeping Tom activities at the top of his lungs.

'Tempest!' exclaimed Amanda from the shower. I glanced back up to find she had turned around and had to avert my eyes again quickly.

'Um, sorry, I didn't realise you were in here,' I backed up to the door, fumbling behind me for the handle as it had swung closed. 'Sorry, I'll be outside.'

Hanging myself.

'Hey, where do you think you are going?' she called after me as she stepped out of the shower. She crossed the room, still naked and dripping wet, her skin glistening with a soapy sheen as she wrapped me into a hug and began kissing me. 'Sorry, I dropped my stupid phone and broke it, or I would have called to let you know I was here.'

'I, ah... I'm all stinky. It's been quite the day.' I said, not wanting to push her away, but not wanting to let her smell me either.

She kissed me again, then took my hand and pulled me, still fully clothed, toward the shower. 'Let's get you clean then.'

The End

Except it isn't there a whole truck load more adventure yet.

Don't miss the fun stuff on the next few pages!

There are secrets buried in the Earth's past. Anastasia might be one of them.

The world knows nothing of the supernaturals among them …

… but that's all about to change.

When Anastasia Aaronson stumbles across two hellish creatures, her body reacts by channelling magic to defend itself and unleashes power the Earth has forgotten.

But as she flexes her new-found magical muscle, it draws the attention of a demon who has a very particular use for her. Now she must learn to control the power she can wield as a world of magical beings take an interest.

She may be damaged, but caught in a struggle she knew nothing about, she will rise, and the demons may learn they are not the real monsters.

The demons know she is special, but if they knew the truth, they would run.

Lord Hale's Monster

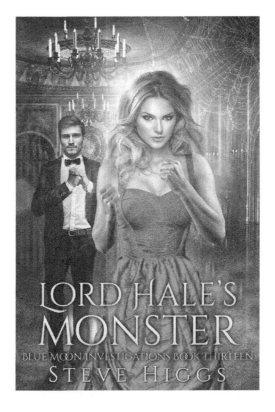

Every second generation of the Hale line dies at the hands of an unnameable monster on his 80th birthday. The current Lord Hale turns 80 this Saturday.

To protect himself, Lord Hale has invited paranormal investigation experts Tempest Michaels and Amanda Harper plus their friends and a whole host of other guests from different fields of supernatural exploration for a birthday dinner at his mansion.

As they sit down for dinner, the lights start to dim and a moaning noise disturbs the polite conversation. Has Lord Hale placed his faith in the right people, or just led them to share his doom?

Finding themselves trapped, Tempest and Amanda, with friends Big Ben and Patience must join forces with a wizard, some scientists, and occult experts, ghost chasers, witches, and other assorted idiots as they fight to make it through the night in one piece.

Could this be their final adventure? Will Tempest finally be proven wrong about the paranormal?

Early Shift

Don't Challenge the Werewolf

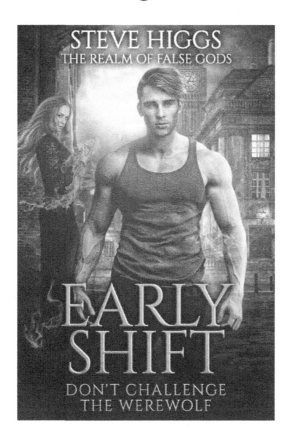

Don't pick a fight with him. You won't lose. You'll die

Zachary has a secret he tries to keep under wraps …

… if only people would let him.

When he drifts into a remote farming community looking for work, the trouble starts before he orders breakfast. Normally he would just avoid the trouble and move on, but there's a girl. Not a woman. A little girl, and the men that want to dominate the village threaten her livelihood.

And that just won't do.

There's something very rotten in this community but digging into it brings him face to face with something more powerful even than him. Something ancient and unstoppable.

He has no choice other than to fight, but who will walk away?

As the false gods find their way into the realm of mortals, how many mortals will rise to defend the Earth?

Be ready for war.

More Books by Steve Higgs

Blue Moon Investigations

Paranormal Nonsense

The Phantom of Barker Mill

Amanda Harper Paranormal Detective

The Klowns of Kent

Dead Pirates of Cawsand

In the Doodoo With Voodoo

The Witches of East Malling

Crop Circles, Cows and Crazy Aliens

Whispers in the Rigging

Bloodlust Blonde – a short story

Paws of the Yeti

Under a Blue Moon – A Paranormal Detective Origin Story

Night Work

Lord Hale's Monster

The Herne Bay Howlers

Undead Incorporated

The Ghoul of Christmas Past

Patricia Fisher Cruise Mysteries

Real of False Gods

Get sneak peaks, exclusive giveaways, behind the scenes content, and more. Plus, you'll be notified of Fan Pricing events when they occur and get exclusive offers from other authors because all UF writers are automatically friends.

Not only that, but you'll receive an exclusive FREE story staring Otto and Zachary and two free stories from the author's Blue Moon Investigations series.

Yes, please! Sign me up for lots of FREE stuff and bargains!

Want to follow me and keep up with what I am doing?

Facebook